Adventures of the Homeless

Adventures of the Homeless

Jagdish R. Singh

iUniverse, Inc.
New York   Bloomington

Adventures of the Homeless

This is a work of fiction. All of the characters, names, incidents, organizations, and dialogue in this novel are either the products of the author's imagination or are used fictitiously.

iUniverse books may be ordered through booksellers or by contacting:

iUniverse
1663 Liberty Drive
Bloomington, IN 47403
www.iuniverse.com
1-800-Authors (1-800-288-4677)

Because of the dynamic nature of the Internet, any Web addresses or links contained in this book may have changed since publication and may no longer be valid. The views expressed in this work are solely those of the author and do not necessarily reflect the views of the publisher, and the publisher hereby disclaims any responsibility for them.

ISBN: 978-0-595-53206-3 (pbk)
ISBN: 978-0-595-63265-7 (ebk)

Printed in the United States of America

iUniverse Rev. 10/29/08

Preface

Adventures of the Homeless is the fourth in a series of books that are based on allegorical, fictional and non-fictional themes, covering a broad range of multicultural issues. The occasional use of the same subject matter is aimed at creating various scenarios of our earthly problems under different circumstances. When analyzing some of these topics, readers are encouraged to follow what their conscience tells them is right and meaningful. Other titles in the series are: The True Self, Earthly Tribulations and Pandora's Heartaches.

CHAPTER 1

━━━━━━━━━━━━━ ▼ ━━━━━━━━━━━━━

It was twilight at the Chelsea Mental Institution when an insane man, tall and heavily built, suddenly entered my room and began calling me a Jewish bastard. Filled with anger and constantly gnashing his teeth, this insane man accused me of abducting his wife and children. Since he was kept under surveillance because of his unpredictable behavior, his unexpected appearance left me stunned, as I could not fathom how he got out of his cell.

Though I was considered mad, like him, I immediately became worried when I saw him shut the door and come toward me with a threatening look. As I slowly retreated, my legs began to quiver and my heart pounded with fear. Suddenly, like a raging bull, the lunatic charged at me, and in a flash he lifted me up and threw me against the window, smashing it open.

Overwhelmed with terror, I instinctively grabbed onto the supporting frame of the window, tightly clinging on to save my life. As I hung out of the tenth floor, I desperately tried to climb back into my room. But he then began to bite my hands like a mad dog. Thinking that I was going to die, there was an astounding change in my fickle mind, as everything that was distressing me quickly vanished. As his teeth sank deeper into my right index finger, I released my hands with the certainty that I was going to die. But just as I felt a chilling sweat amid my fall, something miraculous happened, for I landed on top of a huge maple tree. As I came crashing down through the branches, I desperately tried to cling on to one, and by chance, I managed to grab onto it. I then carefully eased my way through a cluster of leaves to sit on a solid limb. Lowering my head in silence, I thanked the Lord for saving my life.

Seconds later, something out of the blue happened, as my sudden appearance in the tree disrupted a beehive and a few bees darted out to attack me. To stop the rest from coming out of the hive, I quickly took off my shirt and covered the nest. In a jiffy, I tied a knot around it and then hung the nest on a branch. While doing this, I was stung several times by some aggressive bees which I eventually scared away by trying to strike them with my hands.

Looking down below, I saw that my traditional Jewish cap, called a yarmulke, had come off in my fall. I became emotional, for over the years in the asylum, my cap was the only thing that I had which reminded me of my Hebrew faith.

Now that everything appeared fairly calm, I began thinking about what to do. For many years I had been pondering on ways to escape from the Chelsea Mental Institution, and this unfortunate incident of being thrown out the window now seemed favorable. It dawned on me that this was the ideal moment to escape from the asylum, so I decided to remain in the tree until nighttime. As I waited, I reflected on an incident many years ago when I had lost my wife and two children in a tragic fire. It was because of this fatal event that I faced mental torment and suffered two nervous breakdowns. It so distressed me that I later got thrown out of medical school because of my unpredictable behavior and frequent absences. It was when I tried to commit suicide by taking poison, and doctors saved me from dying, that it was decided that I be sent to a mental institution.

Continuing to wait patiently in the tree for the place to become darker, I tried to think of a place to go where no one would recognize me as a mental patient. I was afraid to visit my close relatives, because they were the ones who agreed with the doctors that I be put into an asylum because of my mental illness. Reflecting on places I had visited in the past, a slum area where there were many homeless people suddenly came to mind. I figured that if I lived among them, people might not take too much notice of me, thinking that I too was a homeless person.

Now that it was dark, I decided to throw down my shirt which covered the beehive and then climb down from the tree. My plan was to release the bees on the ground to get back my shirt. With the upper half of my body feeling itchy, I gently rubbed my hands over my face and felt that it had become swollen because the bees had attacked me. My puffed nose and lips, felt as though someone had punched me in the face. Though I was concerned about the swelling, I tried not to lament over it, since finding a place to live was first on my mind.

I climbed down from the tree, looked towards the busy city streets, and saw a small group of people patiently waiting at a bus stop. Seeing a bus approaching, I hurriedly put my hands into my pocket, only to realize that I had no money to board the bus. In desperate need of cash, I decided not to release the bees but approach those who were waiting on the bus and beg them for money. With my shirt off, I honestly felt they would be sympathetic when seeing the lumps on my body. However, they all looked at me with scorn. While pondering on what to do, I saw a few police cars speeding towards the mental institution. Judging from all the excitement, I assumed that I was discovered missing from the asylum.

Seeing the bus was getting closer now, I realized that I had to leave quickly, so I began to plead with an elderly man to give me some money. With my hands outstretched, I closely followed him around, until he eventually gave me three dollars and told me to stop annoying him. I was grateful for this small sum of money since it was enough to allow me to board the bus.

On the bus, I did not want to make anyone uncomfortable, so I decided to sit towards the rear of the vehicle. However, this did not prevent people from taking a brief look at me. Though a few passengers looked at me scornfully, I was not too concerned, thinking that they would not be seeing me again.

Ten minutes later, two teenaged boys boarded the bus and came to sit behind me. From the moment the youths saw the lumps on my body, they began to taunt me. Thinking that I had a strange disease, they yelled at me, "Get off the bus!" Amid it all I remained quiet, since I did not want to get in an argument with them, fearing that any police involvement could lead to me being questioned and sent back to the asylum.

The youths, seeing my yarmulke, soon began to make derogatory remarks about Jews, and this made me feel humiliated. After a while their constant insults about wanting me to get off the bus became unbearable, and slowly I became resentful. Having the beehive still covered with my shirt, my plan was to wait until the bus arrived in the slums and then release the bees on them.

A short while later, the bus stopped and, looking through the window, I saw a group of homeless people. Seeing the two teens and I were the only remaining passengers, I quickly opened the knot on my shirt and threw the beehive at them. As they yelled obscene language and tried to fend off the bees, I hastily jumped off the bus and started to run. At once, the two angry youths came chasing after me. In fear, I ran as fast as I could towards a group of homeless people, screaming for help. Fortunately, when the group saw the youths coming to attack me, they quickly came to my defense, believing the teens were trying to rob me. They began to throw empty liquor bottles and stones at them, and at this sudden attack, the two teens retreated.

As this group of homeless people now gathered around me to find out why these youths were chasing me, I decided to play on their sympathy. I told them the teens had beaten me and robbed me of all the money I had. I also mentioned the youths were coming after me, believing that I had more money hidden on me. The group believed me, and feeling sympathetic, they collectively offered me four dollars and a loaf of bread. I was pleased with their kind offer and their encouraging words of wanting me to join their group. This feeling of importance made me happy after having spent four years feeling dejected in a mental institution.

The area in which I chose to live with this homeless group was called Beaverton. It was a town divided into two sections, one area mainly for the rich and the other largely populated with low-income people. The slums of Beaverton consisted of badly maintained alleys, condemned buildings and narrow streets where prostitutes, drug dealers and homeless people roamed. Though the surrounding area was untidy with litter, it was a place bustling with people commuting. It was common to see people being approached by sellers who had artificial jewelry, clothing and various fruits and vegetables to sell.

After wandering through the streets for a few days, I discovered that most of the homeless people who lived in

Beaverton were not addicted to alcohol or tobacco, because these were two items the majority could not afford. Most of them often visited a nearby shelter for the homeless called Sinai which served two meals each day. Though the Sinai shelter had accommodation for some to sleep at night, the majority chose not to do so, since most of them preferred to be with their own cluster of friends when night fell.

The group I mainly associated with was the same lot who came to rescue me when the youths were chasing me. This group represented a small minority of homeless people who were addicted to alcohol and tobacco. Listening to some of them talk about their early misfortunes, it seemed that they turned to alcohol as a means of suppressing their sorrows.

Here in the ghetto, most of my poor friends often gathered around in the evenings to have friendly talks, and on occasion to exchange food for cigarettes and booze. Later when it became dark, we went our separate ways in dark alleys and at the back of old condemned buildings to rest.

One day as I stood amid the group chatting, a man named Julius who was drunk saw my traditional Jewish cap and addressed me as Rabbi. I was surprised when he called me this, since he did not ask me my name but simply give me one. When the others heard him call me Rabbi, they too began to address me by that title, and from then on it became my nickname. Julius was dressed in black, worn-out clothing, and he had a hammer strapped to his waist. I must say it seemed odd to watch him walking proudly around with it. Since he was drunk, I felt it was not fitting to ask him his reason for carrying a hammer.

While our friendly chat continued, a little person, gently eased his way through the group to introduce himself with a broad smile as Alvis. He declared that he was a wise man who was a follower of the Great King Solomon of the biblical period. Surprisingly, Julius got annoyed and yelled at him, "Go away, and don't bother us with your silly ideas." Alvis quickly changed the subject by asking me if I would like to buy an ounce of marijuana from him, as he had almost one pound to sell. As I was about to say no to Alvis, Julius, in a fit of anger, rudely kicked him on his buttocks and told him to go elsewhere. As Alvis stood confused, an angry Julius reached into his pocket and took out a nail, shouting, "I'll hammer this into your head if you don't leave!" Alvis, seeing Julius untying the hammer that was strapped to his waist, took his threat seriously and remained aloof.

When the rest of the group saw Alvis being mistreated, they all began to laugh and taunt him. I felt sorry for Alvis, who appeared shaken from the blow because he took their insults in silence and slowly walked away from us. This led me to believe the homeless group disliked Alvis, although I could not say whether it was his size, or because of his involvement with illegal drugs.

After one week had passed, Julius introduced me to a man named Lucifer with whom everyone in our group was familiar. I had not met him earlier because he had gone to another part of the city in search of a more favorable place to beg. I learned from Julius that Lucifer came back to rejoin our group after his trip to another district was not productive.

Of all the homeless people in our group, Julius looked the untidiest, for he seldom changed his clothing which were worn-out. The hairs from his nostrils were so long that they almost touched the upper-part of his lip. At times it was nauseating to see him eat, as particles of food often got stuck on the hairs from his nose.

One day as Lucifer, Julius and I were having a friendly chat with others who were homeless, we were taken by surprise to see Alvis slowly walking towards us. From the moment Lucifer saw Alvis, he called him an ass and began shouting at him not to rejoin our group. Annoyed, Alvis stopped and yelled back at Lucifer that he was not coming back to rejoin our group, but wanted to tell me something privately. Before I could say anything on this matter, Lucifer immediately marched towards Alvis, grabbed both of his hands, and began to swing him round and round. Without warning, he suddenly let go of Alvis' hands, causing him to fall abruptly to the ground. Alvis lay on the pavement for a moment, then he slowly sat up, and with a sullen look began to rub his knees vigorously, showing that he was in great pain.

As I watched with pity, Lucifer, Julius and the rest of our homeless friends laughed at Alvis. I began to worry, thinking that he might be severely injured. Alvis looked so dazed after the sudden fall that I felt sympathetic and decided to pick him up. However, as I knelt down to help him, Alvis quietly said to me, "Rabbi, help me get back on my feet that I may walk away from this place and never return."

Julius and Lucifer began shouting at me to leave him; however, since one of his legs was badly bruised, I honestly felt that I could not abandon this injured man. As I tried to help Alvis to walk, he quietly told me not to help him because Lucifer would become more enraged. With a stern look he cautioned me, "Don't trust Lucifer, he is a violent and cunning man."

As Alvis limped away, I asked Julius why everyone in this group hated Alvis so much. Julius, still fuming with anger, claimed that if Alvis continued to sell illegal drugs, the police might one day arrest everyone in their group as accomplices. Though they were right to object to Alvis' illegal doings, I was displeased with the way they treated him, since I honestly felt there were more proper means of getting him to leave.

With Alvis no longer around, Lucifer and Julius looked relieved, for they began to talk about celebrating Alvis' departure with a drink. The two of them were good friends, for Julius opened a bottle of strong liquor and shared it with Lucifer.

Paying much closer attention to Lucifer after Alvis cautioned me about him, I could see that he was a tall, strong man with a commanding voice. At first I could not say much about him, but when he became drunk a few hours later, there was a sudden transformation in his behavior. When Julius and he had finished the bottle of booze, Lucifer became a bully, demanding money from others within our group to buy more alcohol. Listening to him making threatening remarks, I decided to remain silent and not say anything to agitate him.

When Lucifer's hostile behavior towards everyone got to the point where we could no longer bear his insults, the rest of us, including Julius, decided to walk away from him. As we went, Lucifer uttered profane language and called us a bunch of cowards. Our silence in response to Lucifer's verbal abuse was a sign that none of us had the courage to challenge this violent man.

As I walked away feeling embarrassed by Lucifer's insults, Julius called out to say that he was coming to join me. As we casually walked abreast, Julius said, "Lucifer and I had been friends for many years; but his rowdy behavior is becoming unbearable. From this day on I am going to be less friendly with Lucifer, and I'd like the two of us to become better acquainted."

I saw no harm in becoming Julius' friend; however, since he had a hammer strapped to his waist, and had once threatened to strike Alvis with it, I felt unsafe. With an affectionate pat on Julius' shoulder, I politely asked him what was the reason for carrying his hammer around. Julius replied that many had asked the same question before and he told them the hammer was of sentimental value. When I asked the explanation for this, Julius scratched his head, took a deep breath, and brooded over it before saying that at age sixteen he had attended a trade school and later became a skilled carpenter. When he graduated, his father was proud of his achievement, and on his eighteenth birthday his father gave him the hammer as a gift. Julius sorrowfully added that it was while celebrating his eighteenth birthday that his father, who was very overweight, suffered a severe heart attack and died. Deeply saddened by the loss of his father, he fell into a state of despair and spent years lamenting over his father's demise. He then said that this hammer often reminded him of the affection his father had for him.

Feeling touched by what Julius said, I politely asked him to tell me how he became homeless. I learned that he had become angry with his mother, who had found a new male partner only three months after his father had died. Julius said that he was troubled by this and came to dislike his mother. One night he got into a heated argument with his mother over her involvement with the other man, and in anger, she forced him out of the house. Julius went on to say that being unemployed at the time and having nowhere to live, he went into the slums of Beaverton and joined the homeless on the streets. And feeling disheartened in the ghetto, he turned to alcohol as a means of suppressing his sorrows. Having listened to Julius' reason for carrying the hammer around, I felt more at ease, and told him that it was a pleasure to have him as a friend.

*   *   *   *   *

One night as I lay sound asleep on the pavement in front of an old, shabby grocery store, Lucifer, who was drunk at the time, suddenly woke me up, demanding money. Annoyed at being awakened in such a rude manner, I instantly refused and told him to go away. Lucifer became hopping mad and called me a mean Jew, leaving me shocked, as I could not fathom how he knew I was Jewish. It was not until he grabbed my cap and threw it on the ground that I realized the yarmulke I wore led him to this conclusion. Not wanting to get into a fight with him, I did not utter a single word but slowly walked towards my cap to pick it up. However, just as I was about to do so, Lucifer hurriedly stepped on my cap and began stamping on it, shouting derogatory remarks about Jews, making me feel humiliated. Though I was tempted to argue with him, I felt it would be to my disadvantage to settle our dispute with violence, since he was bigger and stronger than me.

As I stood in silence being verbally abused, I recalled the words of my deceased mother who once said to me that hatred for Jews dates back over three thousand years. And even though some still dislike us, I must never instill hatred for anyone in the minds of my offspring. She reminded me not to become revengeful when agonizing over how our ancestors were sold into slavery, for those responsible for such inhumane acts were no longer alive. To her, the way for me to secure a better future was to become educated, and to fulfill my duty in life by doing something good for the betterment of humanity.

While I was lost in thought over these memories, Lucifer realized that I was not angered by his rude comments. He eventually calmed down and slowly walked away. When he was out of sight, I slowly picked up my cap, which was badly soiled, and gently put it into my pocket.

After the incident, it puzzled me as to why none of my homeless friends came out to condemn Lucifer while he was harassing me. I could only guess they had grown accustomed to his rowdy behavior or perhaps they were afraid of him. With everything now seemingly calm, I quietly went back to lie down on the pavement.

Several hours later something unbelievable happened. While sleeping, I suddenly felt drops of water coming down on me. Believing that it was raining, I immediately opened my eyes, and, I was aghast to see Lucifer standing over me and urinating on me. Confused by this filthy act, I hurriedly got up and quickly ran away from him. Lucifer still boiling with rage, shouted, "You are a coward! Go away from here!" Feeling terribly afraid that this man might seriously hurt me, I immediately decided to search for another place to rest.

While hurriedly walking down the alley, I saw Julius totally drunk and searching a pile of garbage for something. The moment Julius saw me he looked happy, and immediately called out for me to come over and have a drink from a bottle of alcohol that he held up with one hand. However, still confused by what Lucifer had done to me, I ignored Julius and hurriedly kept on walking. I deliberated whether to leave this area or not. However, when thinking about going to another place that I was not familiar with, and having to make friends with a new set of homeless people, I decided not to leave.

The following morning, the urine on my clothing gave off an unpleasant smell, and having no additional clothes to wear, I began to think about finding some used clothing. After pondering on this for a while, I decided to visit Julius and beg him for whatever clothing he had.

My journey to find Julius was a short one since he lived in the same alley where I spent the rest of the night after Lucifer had urinated on me. As soon as I got close to Julius who was removing dirt from under his fingernails, he quickly stepped away, telling me how obnoxious I smelled. As I stood aloof with a worrisome look, I began to recount in detail all the terrible things Lucifer had done to me. In the end, Julius became sympathetic and offered me a shirt and a pair of pants that was too big for me. In spite of this, I was grateful since it was something that I desperately needed.

I put on the clothing Julius gave me, but instantly realized that I was going to have problems walking in the oversized pants. However, Julius surprised me when he took off the belt from his pants and fitted it around mine to prevent them from falling down. Calling me Rabbi, Julius with a friendly smile said, "Do not worry for I'm bigger than you and my pants will not fall off that easily." This kind gesture changed my feelings towards Julius, for in the past I always thought of him as a carefree person, but now he showed kindness, a sign that he cared about others.

Leaving Julius, I continued my journey further down the alley in search of somewhere more peaceful to rest. The way Lucifer had humiliated me began to filter through my mind. Brooding over all the embarrassing things he had done to me, and believing that as long as he was around I would be harassed, I started to dislike him.

Since Lucifer was a homeless man, I did not want to physically harm him, thinking that he was probably going through much mental suffering being a frustrated beggar. On the other hand, I was drawn to think that I had to do something unkind to prevent Lucifer from mistreating me. Pondering on this made me vindictive, so I marched over to Lucifer's makeshift tent to let him know that I would no longer put up with his insults. Seeing that he was not at home, I became totally annoyed and angrily tore down his tent. Afterward I felt ashamed but, in my fit of anger to get even with him, I felt that this act was less harmful than physically injuring him.

I began to walk hurriedly down the alley to continue my search for a new home. While rummaging around, I was taken by surprise to see two homeless women sitting in an old abandoned motorcar on a vacant piece of land. As I got closer to them, the elder of the two affectionately asked, "Would you like to go for a drive in our car?" Looking carefully at the vehicle I saw that it had no wheels, and rested on four wooden blocks. Believing that they were trying to make fun of me, I politely refused. However, the elderly woman who sat in the front seat, wearing a purple dress and a white stocking wrapped around her neck, got out of the car and began pleading with me to come with them for a ride. Seeing the pleasant smiles on their faces, I did not want to disappoint them, so I accepted their friendly offer. As I entered the vehicle, I was told to fasten my seat belt, but I chuckled when I saw the car had no seat belts and the two women were going through the motions of putting them on. Seconds later, the elderly woman pretended that she was starting the car, at the same time mimicking the noise of the engine with her mouth. I was immediately drawn to think that both of them had some form of mental illness.

Shortly after, I was told that I had reached my destination, and to my surprise, they asked me to give them two dollars for the ride. Feeling sympathetic because of their mental illness, I gave them two dollars and told them how much I enjoyed the ride. They were absolutely delighted when I gave them the money. The younger woman, constantly smiling at me, happily introduced herself as Sarah. She then invited me to come over to their house, claiming they were having freshly baked bread for dinner. After having been tricked with the car ride, I was reluctant to do so, but considering they were so polite and friendly, I decided to please them by accepting their offer. Surprisingly, after having a casual walk with them for about ten meters, Sarah pointed to their home. Their domain was under the stairs of a shabby, two-storied building. Looking carefully at the part where they lived, I could see that it was well enclosed, for they tied pieces of cardboard around the sides and on a portion of the stairs, to shelter themselves when it rained.

Inside their home, the elderly woman introduced herself as Amelda and whispered in my ear that Sarah was her daughter. She then gave me a bright smile, clearly showing that most of her front teeth were missing. As I stood next to Amelda who gradually inched closer to me, I felt embarrassed when she suddenly pinched me on my buttocks and quietly asked what I thought of Sarah. Not fully understanding what she meant, I tried to be respectful, by telling her that Sarah was a nice person. In a joyful mood, Amelda took out a bottle of wine which she had stored in a small suitcase and offered me a drink. To please her I took one sip and then gave her back the rest. Smiling once more, Amelda slowly lifted the bottle to her mouth and took several gulps. As the excess rich, red wine flowed from her mouth, she occasionally wiped the corners of her jaw with the palm of her hand. She then offered her daughter Sarah one sip from the bottle before closing it and putting it away. Sinking her hands a little deeper into the suitcase, Amelda took out a loaf of bread and divided it among the three of us. As we ate, Amelda constantly talked about the various ingredients she put into the bread to make it tasty. Though it was obvious from the packaging that they had bought the bread from a nearby bakery, I did not dispute her claims. Judging from Amelda and Sarah's behavior, it seemed to me that both of them had found an unusual way to please themselves by using their imagination to create the things they liked.

Hours later, I was taken by surprise when I heard the distant voice of Lucifer yelling as though he were in a fight with someone. As he came storming down the alley ferociously, I could clearly hear him saying that someone had destroyed his home. Soon, he stood right in front of Amelda's place, swearing and complaining about the malicious act. Amelda quickly went outside to calm him down. As I sat quietly inside, knowing that I was the culprit, I felt a bit nervous, thinking that if Lucifer saw me, he would get extremely angry. Amelda was unable to stop Lucifer from swearing, so she hurried back into the house, repeatedly saying to Sarah and me that if Lucifer did not stop, she would physically remove him from in front of her home. When Lucifer continued yelling, Amelda became furious, and told Sarah and me to come out with her and fight Lucifer. Before I could tell her to ignore this violent man, she unexpectedly grabbed my hand and pulled me out of the shelter to confront Lucifer. Upon seeing me, Lucifer became further enraged and started accusing me of destroying his home. With his teeth clenched like a mad dog, he then raised his fist and began threatening to kill me. But as soon as he said this, Amelda and Sarah began to argue with him. Filled with rage, Amelda made it clear that if he hurt me she would kill him. I was absolutely astonished by what this stout, elderly woman said, as I could not believe how humble she was a while ago and how quickly her disposition had changed.

Paying much closer attention to Amelda now, I definitely got the impression that she was tough, for her broad face, thick eyelashes, flared nostrils and missing teeth gave her the look of a fighter. Seeing her trading harsh words with Lucifer, I now realized that Amelda was the no-nonsense type who would not put up with insults from anyone.

A pumped up Amelda told Lucifer that I was innocent, since I was at her place for some time, and someone else must have destroyed his tent. Amid the noisy dispute an elderly man named Sebastian came out of his place and began pleading with us not to be so quarrelsome, or the police would get involved and arrest us all. Sebastian, dressed in khaki clothing, spoke in a humble tone, and he immediately gave me the impression that he was a peaceful person. However, in spite of his plea for us to calm down, much of what he had to say got ignored, as Amelda and Sarah kept on arguing with Lucifer.

As Amelda was constantly shouting and pointing her finger in Lucifer's face, I became astonished when Lucifer suddenly lowered his voice. It was hard to believe that this fiery, elderly woman finally got the six-foot giant Lucifer to speak to her in a more polite manner.

Lucifer was not paying much attention to me now, as he complained to Amelda that he no longer had a place to live. Amelda was understanding and told him not to worry for she would help him in finding one. Now that Lucifer seemed calm, Amelda offered him a can of beer and told him to drink it. This kind gesture softened Lucifer's heart, as he finally became friendlier with us. I then took the opportunity to mention that I did not hate him but would like to have him as a friend. Smiling, he affectionately told me to forget about all our past quarrels.

Reflecting on the dispute we had with Lucifer, I must say that Amelda easily won my heart when she offered Lucifer a can of beer. I came to realize that Amelda was not the spiteful type; instead, she was a frank person who would tell you exactly what she thought. Though one might think of her as abrasive and tactless in her dispute with Lucifer, I felt that deep in her heart she cared about others who were homeless, since she even offered to help Lucifer find a new home.

As Sarah, Amelda, Lucifer and I were having a friendly talk, we were suddenly approached by four policemen. It appeared that someone had informed them about our noisy dispute. Unfortunately, we were all told that we would no longer be allowed to live in this area, and we had forty-eight hours to pack our belongings and leave. The officers then suggested that we go to the Sinai shelter for the homeless, which was a few miles away, for food and refuge.

After the police had left, Amelda and Lucifer made it clear that they would not be going to Sinai. It seemed that they did not want to live in a place with restrictions, having to abide by rules, and not being allowed to smoke or drink alcohol. With all of us in a similar predicament we began deliberating where to go.

Early the following morning I decided to go to another part of the city in search of a place where my friends and I could be together. Having walked for approximately two miles, I saw a huge overpass and decided to go underneath it to see if it was suitable for living. As I stood below, I noticed that there was a wide but shallow stream of running water which flowed under the bridge, and on both sides of the stream there was a dry area of land. This seemed large enough to accommodate my friends, since most of them favored extra space to set up their own little makeshift tent.

While surveying the place, I was delighted to see the surrounding area contained many trees amid areas of rich green vegetation. This made the place isolated and not too visible to the public. Though it was a little noisy under the bridge from the constant flow of traffic above, I felt it was a good place to live, since it was secluded and would shelter us when it rained. Excited with what I saw, I immediately hurried back to tell everyone. Surprisingly, it did not take much to convince Sarah, Amelda and Lucifer to move below the overpass. It seemed that with such short notice by the police to leave, they could not afford to be too selective.

As we began packing our belongings to leave, Julius and Sebastian, who lived nearby, came over to inquire where we were going. When I told them about the new location, both of them readily agreed to join us.

It was under this huge concrete overpass that the six of us lived like a family. Here, we were less concerned about police harassment, thinking that this place was so isolated that there would be fewer complaints from people who disliked our presence.

To aid everyone in getting settled under the bridge, I began to offer help to each of them in setting up their own little area to keep their belongings. Amelda and Sarah were most pleased with my help, as they wanted to enclose a small area under the bridge using pieces of cardboard, which they brought with them. I must say that it took them almost two days to complete their makeshift tent, as they had to remove most of the cardboard from their old home and fetch it below the bridge.

While helping Sebastian and Julius to clear a small area where they could set up their tents, I was disappointed to see Lucifer standing aloof and scratching his armpit while the rest of us were cleaning the area. Knowing how arrogant and lazy he was, I decided to remain quiet and not ask what was irritating him.

Having helped the others in setting up their tents, I decided to ask Lucifer if he needed my help in setting up his, but Lucifer left me astonished by telling me that he did not want any help from a Jew. I immediately realized that all along Lucifer was pretending to be friendly on the surface, while deep in his heart he harbored hatred for me. Being afraid of this man, I allowed him to pitch his tent wherever he pleased. But unfortunately for him, the location he chose was only twelve feet away from where Amelda and Sarah had pitched their tent. When Amelda saw Lucifer setting up his tent next to her, she became furious and called him an obstinate fool. She said she could not tolerate him living next to her and demanded that Lucifer choose another spot. As Amelda walked up and down yelling insults at Lucifer, I was surprised once more when I saw him refraining from arguing with her. With a disappointed look, he quietly muttered something before picking up his belongings to move to another location.

The following day, Sebastian surveyed the area. He pointed out that the place where we now lived was far from the heart of the city, and it was going to be a difficult task to cover the distance each day. He said that to make it less arduous it would be to our advantage to go to the Sinai shelter and ask for some of the canned food and clothing that were donated by people. He believed that by occasionally doing this, we would not have to go out begging each day. This did not seem like a good idea to Amelda, Lucifer and Julius for they quickly opposed him. Meanwhile, Sarah and I, who were listening attentively to Sebastian, realized that what he had said made sense, so we began pleading with the others to go to Sinai. This was not easy, for it took the two of us almost an hour to convince them how important it was to set aside some food in the event that we got too little from begging on some occasions. After pleading with them for some time, they finally agreed, and the six of us headed for Sinai.

Arriving at the Sinai shelter, Sebastian and I were taken aback when the security officer who was standing at the main entrance refused to allow Julius, Amelda and Lucifer to enter the building. The officer claimed the three of them had been warned several times before not to come to Sinai because of the number of disputes they had with guards and other homeless people when drunk. Sebastian and I now understood why Julius, Amelda and Lucifer were so adamant about not going to Sinai. When Lucifer was repeatedly told to leave he became furious, and in a fit of anger, he punched the guard on the nose. Seconds later three other security men were called in to help. They quickly pounced on Lucifer and forced him to leave. After this, the guard who was punched on the nose called us all a mischievous bunch and warned us not to come back to the Sinai shelter.

As we all began our journey home, feeling disgruntled after the unpleasant incident, Sebastian paused for a moment to look at Lucifer, and then shook his head as if to say Lucifer had ruined his credibility. I got the impression that Sebastian was concerned about associating with a violent man like Lucifer, probably fearing that Lucifer might one day be in conflict with the law, and he might be accused of being his accomplice.

The next day, we all returned to our daily task of walking great distances begging for money. On each of our travels to the city I made it a habit to stay close to Amelda and Sarah, for I had this phobia that Lucifer might step up from behind and strike me. I was not the aggressive type and knew one thing for sure, that as long as Amelda was near me, Lucifer would not quarrel with me since he was afraid of her bullish attitude. Though he was a strong and powerful man, I felt that he was hesitant to strike Amelda, knowing that if he ever did so, he would be hated by everyone.

Returning home after a long and tiresome walk, most of us were pleased with the little money we got from begging. However, on this day, Lucifer returned home empty-handed. Frustrated, he began complaining that for the whole day he was out begging, no one gave him any money. Thinking that by ignoring him he might eventually calm down, we were all taken by surprise when Lucifer started to make threatening remarks, and demanded that we give him some money. Believing that this crazy man might want to hurt one of us, I offered him four dollars. Without hesitating, Lucifer quickly took the coins, but just as he was about to put them into his pocket, he paused for a moment to think. Suddenly, he became reddened with anger and then threw the money back at me, claiming that he could not accept handouts from a Jew. As I slowly lowered my hands to pick up the scattered coins, Amelda, who had been struggling to control her anger, became furious and began scolding him for being so inconsiderate.

Their confrontation soon turned into a heated argument, and in the middle of it, Lucifer shoved Amelda to the ground. As Amelda rubbed her buttocks and tried to get back on her feet, Lucifer knocked her down a second time by cruelly kicking her in the stomach. Julius, who was in sober thoughts that day, became hopping mad and began to throw stones at Lucifer. While Sarah impulsively rushed to help her injured mother, Sebastian and I immediately joined Julius in stoning Lucifer. As Lucifer was hit with a barrage of stones, it suddenly ceased when Sarah began pleading with us not to harm Lucifer. This infuriated me as I could not comprehend how Sarah could leave her injured mother who was the victim in this incident and show compassion for the evildoer. While Sebastian, Julius and I began to question Sarah about her protecting Lucifer, we were left with our mouths agape when Lucifer called us all a bunch of cowards and then hurriedly left the area.

With Lucifer not around, Sarah sobbed that she was a softhearted person and could not bear witness to someone being punished for their wrongdoings. Seeing her so distraught, I decided not to question her or say anything to further distress her. As Sebastian and I calmed Sarah, Julius, who in the meantime was helping Amelda to get back on her feet, called out to Sarah to come over and help him to take Amelda back to her makeshift tent. When the three of them had left, I quietly asked Sebastian if he could tell me the reason why Sarah had neglected her own mother, who was a victim of abuse, and instead protected the attacker. Sebastian replied that this is a form of weakness on the part of many who are caring or softhearted. He believed that such people, having a forgiving disposition, seem to care less about upholding what is fair or just. Sebastian then boldly claimed that most compassionate or righteous people seem to lack balanced judgment, for when they are asked to deal with crimes against humanity they do not want to get involved. What happened this day made me realize that amid my belief in peace and forgiveness, I also had to bear in mind how to deal with those who do not believe in peace and are determined to harm the innocent.

Now that Lucifer was no longer around, we all felt relieved, for his despotic ways were making us feel uneasy. In days to follow we were much united and seemed more like a family. Though there were sporadic quarrels between Julius and Amelda over trivial matters, they were never vindictive, but were quick to rekindle their friendship. Their disputes usually came about when Amelda often complained that Julius' loud snoring was interrupting her sleep at night.

From the time we came to live under the bridge, it was common at night to see Julius lying on his back and sleeping with his mouth open. Amelda was sure that this was causing him to snore heavily. For some time she wanted Julius to move to a distant corner under the bridge, but he had grown to like a particular spot and was determined not to move. Amid the minor fallouts between Amelda and Julius, there were occasions for Sebastian and me to smile, for it was amusing to see the frolics of Amelda, as she occasionally marched up and down before going to bed at night, cautioning Julius not to snore. Then amid her fret, Julius would affectionately put his arm around her and offer her a drink. Julius knew Amelda had a weakness for alcohol, and it was pleasing to see them reconcile after an earlier dispute and sing love songs that they made up.

One week after Lucifer had left, I experienced one of the most unpleasant moments in my life. And it was from this incident that I developed a compassionate feeling for my homeless friends. While begging when it was hot and enervating, I became worried that after three hours in the sweltering heat no one offered me any money. After awhile I began to feel hungry, and soon I was in desperate need of something to eat. With sweat dripping from my forehead, my lips and throat became dry and I felt as if I were going to faint. Looking wearily around, I saw a man selling food in a mobile vehicle. I immediately became excited, and with the little strength I had, tried my utmost to get close to him to beg for something to eat. Unfortunately, when I told the man that I had no money, he became angry and yelled at me to beg elsewhere. At this point I did not have enough strength to keep on pleading with him, so I slowly turned and walked away.

About to collapse at any moment from hunger, I gently lowered myself to the ground to avoid falling suddenly. Out of the blue, I heard the voice of Julius, who was drunk, calling out to me to come and have a drink with him. Julius, seeing me on the ground and not responding to his call, staggered towards me to ask what was wrong. Seeing him holding a bottle of wine, I signaled with my hand for him to give me some of it. As usual, Julius was happy to do so, and taking the bottle from him, I began to drink it ravenously. Watching me take gulps of it, Julius looked astonished, since I had always refused him in the past. Minutes later, I began to feel a little better, and amid this feeling I took an oath that if I were ever to become wealthy, I would buy a mobile vehicle and serve a free meal to the homeless in Beaverton each day. What had happened to me this day was unforgettable, for I could never imagine that hunger could debilitate me to the point where my entire body felt powerless.

Julius was still puzzled by my strange behavior, so I explained how hungry I was and how relieved I felt when he offered me a drink. Though Julius was drunk at the time, he seemed concerned, as he was attentive to what I had to say. He affectionately told me not to worry, for he would follow me home and ensure that I got something to eat.

Arriving home, Julius immediately told Sebastian that I was not well, and to bring me something to eat. Sebastian, sensing that it was urgent, hastily opened a bag he often wore around his shoulder, and took out an apple which he insisted that I eat. Feeling a lot better after eating, I expressed sincere thanks to both of them. Julius, seeing that I was okay now, returned to his place to rest, saying he would come back later to see me.

With Julius not around, Sebastian began to inquire about what had happened to me. Once again I had to recount the experience of having no money and being in desperate need of food. Sebastian gave me a pleasant surprise when he opened his bag once more, took out a handful of coins and gave them to me, saying that he did not want me to experience such hunger again. I became lost as to how to respond, since I honestly felt there weren't enough words to express my gratitude. This kind gesture made me realize that Sebastian was a true friend who not only held me in high esteem but also cared about me.

Soon it was sunset and, while sitting alone reflecting on what had happened to me earlier that day, I saw Amelda cautiously walking around a tree that was about twenty meters from where I sat. Being inquisitive, I decided to move a little closer to see what she was doing. Peeking between the limbs of another tree, I saw Amelda catch a small lizard from a branch and quickly put it into a glass jar. Seeing that what she did was of little importance, I decided to remain hidden and allow her to go back to her place without saying anything to her.

Later when the place got much darker, I decided to join the others in taking an early rest. However, this night I found it difficult to sleep, as my mind was active, constantly rehearsing the events of the day. While lying with my eyes open, I saw Amelda quietly coming out of her place with one hand on top of the glass jar and the other below. She then tiptoed cautiously towards Julius, and in a flash, she took the lizard out of the jar and dropped it into Julius' open mouth.

Seconds later, Julius began to cough and upon opening his eyes, he saw Amelda standing over him and yelling at him to swallow. With Julius seemingly choking, Amelda quickly ran down to the stream and filled the jar with water. She hurried back and offered it to Julius who began drinking to clear his throat. Amid the excitement, Sarah and Sebastian came rushing towards Julius to find out what had happened. However, before Julius could say anything, Amelda quickly interrupted to say that she was coming out of her tent to get some water when she suddenly saw a lizard on Julius' forehead, then as she got closer to scare the reptile away, it ran into Julius' mouth and went down his throat. I knew this was a lie, for I saw Amelda put the lizard in Julius' mouth herself. Since everyone else including Julius was not sure about what had happened, they all believed Amelda's story. At this point I realized that it would be unfitting to dispute Amelda's claims, because if I did, there would be a bitter dispute between Julius and Amelda. While Julius was still stunned by what had happened, Amelda took the opportunity to remind him not to sleep with his mouth open. This made me realize that Amelda intended to put an end to Julius' snoring, although I could not tell whether the silly thing she did might be from malice or out of frustration.

For the remainder of the night, none of us slept as we kept discussing what had happened to Julius over and over again. Amid all this talk, Julius appeared distressed by the fact that he had swallowed a lizard that was alive. And to add to his worry, Amelda kept on telling him if he had listened to her and closed his mouth when sleeping, this incident would never have occurred. It was pleasing that her daughter Sarah, who knew absolutely nothing about what her mother had done, was polite to Julius, telling him not to worry for he would eventually overcome the unpleasant happening. Unfortunately, after she said this, Julius got the hiccups which added to his discomfort even more. To console him at a time when he looked so down-spirited, a softhearted Sarah gently rubbed his back, saying affectionately to him that she was prepared to stay awake all night until he felt better.

Soon it was the break of dawn, and by now one would have expected Julius to be in better spirits, but he was still depressed. Amelda was in a joyful mood, thinking the silly thing she did might put an end to Julius' snoring. She told Sebastian and me not to keep on agonizing over Julius' problem, claiming that she knew what to do to make him happy. To my surprise, she went into her tent and brought out a bottle of liquor, and with a bright smile she offered it to Julius. However, she was astonished when Julius refused, claiming the alcohol would make him feel worse. Disappointed, Amelda called Julius a fool, and to further annoy him, she took two gulps from the bottle and angrily walked back to her tent. A concerned Sebastian told Sarah and me to leave Julius alone, as he needed some time to get over the unpleasant incident.

Hours later, Julius was in a better mood, probably realizing that it was useless to keep on lamenting. Surprisingly, he went to Amelda of his own accord and politely asked for some of her booze. Once again, Amelda showed that she was not the kind to remain spiteful forever, for she willingly gave Julius what he requested. The day ended on a pleasant note, for Julius appeared happy and, once again, he and Amelda sang their favorite songs while intoxicated.

In days to follow, Julius was back to his usual self, continuing to drink and snore heavily at nights, as well as having minor disputes with Amelda. However, just as Julius seemed to have overcome the unpleasant experience of swallowing a lizard, he came upon another distressing incident. While drinking with Amelda and Sarah, he became drunk and told Sarah that he was going to swim in the stream below the bridge.

When Julius got close to the stream, he saw a school of small fish and became excited. Believing that he could catch some of them, he suddenly ran into the water to grab some of the fish. But he inadvertently slipped and fell, striking his forehead on a rock below the water.

No one witnessing his sudden fall, Julius lay unconscious in the water. It was not until Sarah began yelling for him to come back and join them, and did not get a response, that she decided to go by the stream to see what he was doing. Sarah discovered Julius lying face down in the water, and with a frantic cry for help, she quickly rushed into the stream and began dragging Julius out of the water. As soon as the rest of us heard Sarah's frantic cry, we hurriedly ran down to the stream. By the time we got there, Sarah had just pulled Julius out of the water. In panic, she pleaded with us to do something to prevent Julius from dying. I quickly told her to calm down and allow me to check his pulse. Fortunately, I felt it beating and immediately I turned him on his side to begin the process of reviving him. But just as I did this, Amelda came rushing towards me, claiming that she could perform a miracle and save Julius from dying. Sarah immediately fell into a state of despair and began calling on the Lord to save Julius. Her constant pleas irritated her mother, and with a sudden outburst of rage, Amelda yelled at her, "Shut up!"

For a brief moment I was taken aback by Amelda's rude remark; then, as I turned away from her to begin reviving Julius, she suddenly came from behind and pushed me out of the way. As I looked in awe, Amelda gave me a stunning surprise when she rolled Julius onto his back, and without uttering a word of caution, she unexpectedly jumped with both of her feet on top of Julius' stomach. With the sudden impact, almost a pint of water flew out of his mouth, and a painful look appeared on his face. Seconds later, when Julius opened his eyes and moved his hands, Amelda became totally convinced that she had brought Julius back to life. Confused by it all, I could not decide whether to argue with Amelda or not, for I was happy to see Julius alive. I do not advise anyone to attempt what Amelda did to Julius, because not only was it fortuitous, but also I had already checked his pulse and knew he was alive.

Soon Julius became more composed and slowly he walked towards Sarah to thank her for saving his life. When Amelda heard this she became outraged, and began to march up and down, claiming that she was the one who saved Julius' life and not her daughter. An angry Amelda pointed out that everyone saw when she jumped on Julius' stomach, and why should he thank Sarah for saving his life. Julius, seeing how agitated Amelda was, explained that while he lay face down in the water, he witnessed something startling: he felt completely separated from his body, and could actually see Sarah pulling his body out of the water. Amelda became more agitated as she stamped her foot on the ground and hurriedly walked away from us.

As Sebastian and I pondered on what Julius said, Amelda suddenly returned and dealt Julius a hard blow to the head with a frying pan. As we all looked in awe, Amelda told Julius the conk on his head was to remind him that she was the one who saved his life. Sarah became furious and began to quarrel with her mother for being so silly. While they argued, Julius looked bewildered as he watched their noisy dispute in silence.

This dispute between Amelda and Sarah was bitter since both of them had harsh words to say to each other. Sarah in particular was argumentative, telling her mother to shut her big mouth, since the blow to Julius's head could have easily put him into an unconscious state once more. It took much pleading on the part of Sebastian and me to stop their heated argument.

When Sarah and Amelda had stopped quarreling and had returned to their places, Sebastian and I decided to stay with Julius until he became fully composed. Julius took both of us by surprise when he turned to me and said, "Rabbi, do you believe that one's personality-self dies after the death of their physical body?" I was surprised when Julius asked this question, since he was a nonchalant person who never had any religious concerns. In reply, I told Julius that I could not answer this question with certainty; however, my religious beliefs guided me to think of a God with Whom I wished to live in peace after death. Julius, not convinced by my answer, then turned to Sebastian to ask the same question. Unlike me, Sebastian did not give an outright answer; instead, he questioned Julius as to why he needed to know if there was life after death. Julius explained that while he lay unconscious in the water, he was absolutely certain that he was out of his body, claiming he actually saw Sarah struggling to pull his body out of the water. Sebastian responded that the feeling of being separated from his physical body was a near-death experience. He advised Julius not to be too concerned about life after death, since he would never meet face to face with the Almighty. Julius, not getting a clear answer, left to change his wet clothing. Shortly after this, Sebastian and I returned to our places to relax for a while.

While sitting alone, I began to reflect on the misfortunes some of my homeless friends and I had experienced. In a compassionate frame of mind, I honestly felt that there was something I could do to extricate my friends from poverty.

In retrospect, I could never have imagined that I would become a beggar, for I was fairly wealthy prior to the misfortunes I had met. Under these circumstances, money was probably the most important means of changing my status in life. I thought that if I saved enough of it, I might one day be able to start a business of my own. And with the profit I made, I could give some financial help to the homeless. This, however, was wishful thinking, for the money I got from begging was just enough to provide me with the little food that I needed to survive.

CHAPTER 2

▼

After a month had passed, we were all astonished one day to see Lucifer standing approximately thirty meters from where we lived. Believing he was coming to attack us, we quickly began to gather up stones to throw at him. Upon seeing this, Lucifer quickly said, "Rabbi, I need your help." I told the others not to stone him, but wait until I found out what he wanted from me. Lucifer looked pale, and seemed to have lost a considerable amount of weight. With a somber expression, Lucifer said politely that he was hungry and would like to come back and live with us. Seeing him so distraught and in poor health, I became sympathetic and pleaded with the others to let him rejoin our group. This was not easy because Amelda, Sarah and Julius were against allowing him to stay, since they did not trust him. It was not until Sebastian intervened and told them that everyone deserved a second chance, and that Lucifer was more humble now than ever, that they agreed to let him rejoin our group. Looking at Lucifer, who appeared in poor health, I was drawn to think that because he was a lazy and violent person, it would be difficult for him to survive on his own. Though he had insulted me a great deal in the past, I could not remain spiteful, because I was the forgiving type.

In the coming weeks, Lucifer regained his strength after we had allowed him to eat well and to take plenty of rest. During his illness, he never drank any alcohol and was much friendlier with me. One day, when he had a more peaceful disposition, I asked him why he despised me so much. In reply, Lucifer claimed that he was not racist, and the reason he disliked me was because I did not support him whenever he got into a dispute with others. For a brief moment I was taken aback, but when considering how much friendlier he had become, I was cheerfully optimistic, believing that he had come to realize that I was not an evil person.

After my conversation with Lucifer, I happily mentioned to Sebastian how pleased I was that Lucifer no longer disliked me. However, despite my optimism, Sebastian cautioned me not to trust Lucifer's claim that he was not racist. He said that while it was my wish to see Lucifer do well, such an envious and spiteful person would want to see me fail in life.

Displeased with what Sebastian said, I fervently asked, "What kind of a man would I be if I could not forgive or trust Lucifer, now that he seems humble?" Sebastian replied that though it might sound unfair, I should always maintain a scintilla of caution and not put my entire trust in anyone, since I would never be able to tell the kind of feelings a friend or foe silently harbored for me. Speaking in broader terms, Sebastian stated that an individual like Lucifer, who was poorly educated and had less concern for moral values, tended to have the attitude of a bully. He believed that such people are likely to envy the success of those who are hard working, and when faced with hardships, they have a tendency to rob or take advantage of them. Sebastian claimed that it could be misleading for Lucifer or anyone else to say that they do not have any prejudice for others of a different race or religion. He made the point that even the ancient prophets and millions who glorify the name of God have harbored prejudiced feelings towards those who did not support their beliefs.

As Sebastian kept on trying to convince me not to trust Lucifer, I quietly held on to my belief that to live in harmony with Lucifer, I had to be polite and encourage him to become a better person. Thus I cautioned Sebastian not to be too judgmental, as I honestly believed that there are many people who sincerely care for others regardless of their beliefs or color. Sebastian replied that even such people whom I considered good could develop biased feelings when others of a different race occasionally mistreat them or people of their own kind. Sebastian went on to say that what prevents prejudice from exacerbating are the laws aimed to stem the flow of discrimination, and the tolerance and respect most of us have for others. At this point I realized that my conversation with Sebastian was becoming more and more complicated, since both of us were equally determined to convince each other what we felt was right. In the end, I told Sebastian that it was only fair that I encourage Lucifer to change for the better and not to hold any grudge against him.

Unfortunately, this optimistic feeling I had that Lucifer would improve was short lived, for he soon developed a habit of not going out to beg. I observed that while the rest of us were out each day begging, Lucifer chose to remain under the bridge until we returned with food. Though he looked in much better health, he claimed that he had developed stomach problems, and was not well enough to go out and beg. Knowing the kind of person he was, I became suspicious that he was pretending to be ill. However, I did not share this suspicion with the others, believing they might insult him if they found out.

A week later, after Lucifer was alone while the rest of us were out, we all returned to find Lucifer drunk. An angry Amelda, wanting to know where he got alcohol from, hurried into her tent and discovered her liquor missing. Infuriated, she instantly accused Lucifer of stealing her liquor and demanded that he leave immediately. Lucifer got angry and began swearing at her. Witnessing his rude behavior, we quickly realized that all of us had been misled by his malingering. On this occasion our confrontation with Lucifer was short, for from the moment he saw us gathering stones to throw at him, he decided to leave of his own accord.

Days later when all seemed back to normal, Amelda approached me, asking that I come to her tent for she had something important to discuss with me. Curious, I followed her. When I entered her place, I was taken by surprise to see Sarah sitting on the ground, constantly smiling at me. As I looked around for a place to sit, Amelda quickly asked me to sit next to Sarah. She then opened a box which contained many coins and offered it to me. When I began to protest her generosity in wanting to give me some of the money she had saved over the years, she quietly said to me that Sarah was in love with me and wanted me to marry her. Sarah appeared happy, and with a charming smile, she slowly reached out to touch my right hand. Then she gently folded her hands around mine like a glove.

Sarah seemed much the opposite of her mother, for she was fairly tall and looked well in her face for someone who had a hard life and wore no make-up. She had beautiful blue eyes and a youthful body with breasts that looked full and round. However, in spite of her physical attributes, I had no lustful desires or amorous feelings for her. Considering that she was suffering from some form of mental illness, I honestly felt it was wrong to deceive her.

As I sat thinking about what to say, Amelda came closer to me and whispered in my ear, "All this money could be yours if you marry Sarah." Since I had been a married man who became separated from my wife after she died, I immediately made them aware of this. I politely explained that I could not marry her because we were both homeless, and the responsibilities of marriage would put too much strain on our lives. Sarah was disappointed and began to cry. Realizing that she had mental problems, I tried to calm her down by telling her that she was beautiful and that she would surely get married someday. To comfort her, I gently put my arm around her shoulder, but she became furious and hastily ran out of the tent, claiming that she was going to jump off the bridge above us and kill herself. I became afraid and ran after her. Seeing the distraught look on Sarah's face and the direction she was heading, it seemed clear to me that she was going to kill herself.

Pleading with Sarah not to take her own life, Amelda quickly came running after me, saying, "If my daughter commit suicide, you will be responsible for her death." With the pressure now mounting on me to stop Sarah, I repeatedly shouted that I would marry her. Sarah instantly stopped running, dried her tears and smiled at me joyfully. Before I could give her a hug to comfort her, Amelda came up from behind and demanded that Sarah and I get married immediately before I changed my mind. Amelda appeared restless, for she often pushed her right hand into her bosom to pull up the strap on her bra. It seemed that while running after me and every so often gesticulating, her bra had come loose.

While heading back to our places, I began to think how unfortunate it was for me to keep the promise of marriage to someone I was not in love with. However, it soon dawned on me not to be excessively concerned since the marriage would not be legitimate, and I was only doing this to prevent Sarah from committing suicide.

As we returned under the bridge, Sebastian and Julius immediately began to inquire what all the excitement and screaming were about. Amelda quickly told them not to worry for she had good news, that Sarah and I would be getting married today and the two of them were invited to bear witness to the marriage. Sebastian and Julius were excited when they heard the announcement, and within minutes, they began to help Amelda in gathering up pieces of wood to make a bench for Sarah and me to sit on. Here, Julius was helpful as he quickly took out his hammer and began nailing pieces of wood together. As soon as this was done, Sebastian asked Amelda where the priest was to perform the wedding. Amelda stopped briefly to think, and then quickly announced that Sebastian would be the officiating priest. Seeing Sebastian totally puzzled by this, I quickly approached him and whispered to go ahead and perform the wedding, since I was only doing this to stop Sarah from committing suicide. Sebastian was understanding and decided to proceed with the wedding. He then gave a short speech and made us exchange vows before declaring Sarah and me husband and wife. This was pleasing to Amelda, and immediately after the short ceremony, she opened a bottle of wine and shared it with everyone.

In the coming weeks, Sarah was attentive and treated me with kindness. Her mother moved out of the makeshift tent that she shared with Sarah and pitched another approximately thirty feet away, to allow Sarah and me to be together. In this relationship with Sarah, I tried my utmost not to say anything to distress her, knowing how unpredictable she could become when displeased. Since she had some form of mental illness, I did not want to take advantage of her by uniting with her in sex. However, this turned out to be a big problem for me, for after one week, she began to complain to her mother about me not wanting to touch her. This made Amelda angry, and instead of meeting with me somewhere else to discuss this matter, she marched into the tent when I was alone and suddenly grabbed my testicles, demanding that I use them because Sarah wanted to have children. My eyes became watery from the sharp pain and when I could no longer bear it, I gave in to her request. It was a painful experience, for even after Amelda had released her hands, I had to sit like a woman with my legs crossed for several minutes until the pain lessened. It was also worrisome for me, knowing that I was being encouraged to have sex with a woman whom I was not in love with or legally married to.

A few hours after this unpleasant incident, I politely asked Sarah to go with me for a leisurely walk in the city. My intention was to discuss with her in a rational manner what marriage really meant.

On our journey, Sarah made a sudden stop by a busy marketplace when she saw a teenage boy selling apples, and began pleading with me to purchase some. As we both approached the lad to ask the price of the apples, we noticed that he had a monkey helping him by taking the apples out of a box and placing them on a wooden table. I was impressed by how clever and obedient the monkey was when told what to do.

When Sarah asked for the price of the apples, she was surprised when the lad told her that he would give them to her for free, and she could take as many as she wanted. Immediately, Sarah got excited and without uttering a word of thanks, she began picking up the apples, while the teenage boy happily introduced himself as Reuben. Judging from the way Reuben was looking and smiling at Sarah, I got the feeling that he had fallen in love with her.

After Sarah had finished selecting the fruits and was about to leave, Reuben surprised both of us once more when he affectionately said to Sarah that she could visit him each day for fresh apples. Sarah was overjoyed when she heard this and promised to come back whenever she needed more apples. As I was about to leave with Sarah, Reuben quickly approached me to ask if he could have a private talk with me. I was astonished when he asked me if I was married to Sarah. When I told him that I was not, he immediately pleaded with me to tell Sarah that he was in love with her. Reuben appeared young, so I politely asked him his age. When he mentioned that he was only fourteen, I immediately told him that he was too young for Sarah, who was more than twice his age.

Sarah, who had been waiting patiently, then interrupted us by calling out to me that it was time to leave. Unaware of what we were discussing, she politely said to Reuben that he could continue his conversation with me the following day because she would be coming back for more apples.

On our way home, Sarah pleaded with me to stop for a moment when she saw a mid-sized garbage container. Without saying anything, she began searching amid the garbage, hoping to find something of value. As I waited patiently, she hurried to show me a doll which she found in the trashcan. I became astonished when Sarah affectionately embraced the doll and claimed it to be her child. Though I was puzzled by the affection she was showing the doll, I did not prevent her from doing so, believing that if she became attached to the doll, she would be less attentive to me.

When we returned home later that day, I felt relieved, for Sarah became less attentive to me and began to spend more time with the doll. Fortunately, she never again complained to her mother about me not wanting to share the same bed with her. What turned out to be even more puzzling was that Amelda, who had a similar mental illness as Sarah, happily accepted the doll as her grandchild and began treating it as if it were an infant. Though I felt relieved when the two of them were no longer so attentive to me, I was saddened to think that both might be in a state of mental decline.

Two days later, Sarah came to me asking that I accompany her to get more of the apples Reuben had promised her. I immediately agreed, knowing how moody she could become if turned down. At the market place, Reuben was very attentive to Sarah, helping her in selecting those fruits that looked almost perfect. After Sarah had selected about a dozen apples, she told Reuben to keep them because she wanted to go to another seller who had some of the finest necklaces displayed in an open showcase.

As Sarah looked at the jewelry, the owner of the booth, recognizing us as homeless people, immediately began yelling at us to go elsewhere. Trying to sway Sarah from getting into an argument over something so trivial, I quickly told her that it was not worthwhile looking at the jewelry because neither of us could afford to buy it. After a short deliberation, she agreed to go back to Reuben to take the fruits he had given her and leave. However, when Sarah came to Reuben to pick up the fruits, she began to complain to him how unkind the owner of the jewelry stall was when he yelled at her. She said to Reuben that she had always wanted a gold necklace but could not afford one. Surprisingly, Reuben, wanting to please Sarah, told her to come back the following day, and he would buy her a necklace. Sarah was in awe when she heard this, as she could not understand why the lad was so kind to her, and willing to do almost anything to make her happy.

Looking at Reuben who was poorly clad, I could not fathom where he was going to get the money to buy the necklace for Sarah. I decided to question him about it. Not wanting Sarah to hear, I told her to take the apples home and I'd meet her later. To encourage her to leave, I told her that I wanted to spend some time with Reuben so we could become more acquainted with each other.

After Sarah had left, I quickly approached Reuben to find out where he was going to get the money to buy the necklace. I learned that both of his parents had died in a car accident, and his grandfather had given him his mother's wedding ring to keep. He affectionately said that he was going to give the ring to Sarah as a gift.

Saddened about the death of his parents, I began to express my sympathy. However, Reuben interrupted me by saying that he did not want to spend too much time discussing this subject because it was making him emotional.

Realizing that the ring he wanted to give to Sarah was of sentimental value, I began to plead with him not to give it to her, since it could occasionally bring back loving memories of his deceased mother. This was not enough to get Reuben to change his mind, for he told me that he would not mention the ring once belonged to his mother, but would tell Sarah that he bought it for her. Reuben said that he was sure that when Sarah saw the ring, she would show more affection for him and slowly he was going to win her heart. Seeing how determined Reuben was to please Sarah, I did not want to say anything to annoy him or make him feel that he was not good enough for Sarah. So I told him that it was time for me to leave and that Sarah and I would come back the next day to visit him.

The following day, Sarah encouraged me to go with her to meet Reuben who had promised her a necklace. Knowing that Reuben was going to give her a ring instead, I tried my utmost to discourage her from meeting him. Sarah, however, was persistent, for she kept telling me the necklace would not only make her look beautiful, but it would become the most valuable thing she ever owned. Thinking about Sarah's mental condition and how angry she could become when she did not get what she strongly desired, I decided to accompany her to meet Reuben.

At the market place, Reuben was happy to see Sarah. Surprisingly, on this occasion he said to her, "I am in love with you, and I want to marry you." Such caring words, however, did not impress Sarah since she was more interested in the necklace that he had promised. Reuben, slowly reaching into his pocket, then took out the ring and offered it to her. Sarah, looking unhappy, immediately claimed that it was not what she wanted. She handed back the ring to Reuben and raised her voice to tell him to sell it, and use the money from the sale to buy her a necklace. At this point I silently began deliberating what to say to both of them. On one hand, I was displeased with Reuben for wanting to give away a ring that was of sentimental value, and on the other hand, when thinking about Sarah's mental condition, I did not know how to let her understand that she was putting too much pressure on this lad to provide her with an expensive gift. While I pondered, Reuben told Sarah and me to come back later in the day because he was going to sell the ring and use the money to buy a necklace for Sarah. Hearing this, Sarah looked pleased and immediately began urging me to leave and to come back later.

As I stood with Sarah deliberating where to go next, we were both left aghast when a stray dog suddenly appeared and charged after Reuben's monkey. Terrified, the monkey hastily ran over to the neighboring jewelry stall and jumped into the glass showcase that contained many expensive necklaces. When the owner of the booth saw the monkey in his showcase, he tried to chase away the animal, but the monkey, feeling cornered, quickly buried its head between the necklaces. Seconds later, the frightened animal ran out of the showcase and hurried back to Reuben with a necklace inadvertently hung around its neck. Reuben quickly took the necklace off the monkey's neck and began to admire it. Then both Sarah and I were in shock when the owner of the jewelry stall came over, and began accusing Reuben of sending his monkey to steal the necklace from his booth. As Sarah and I were about to argue with the owner for wrongfully accusing Reuben, the stray dog returned once more, and made an impetuous dash towards the monkey. Terrified, the monkey hastily ran up a light-pole to escape. As the distressed animal struggled to climb along the thin electrical wires, it became more terrified when its entire body moved convulsively. While we looked on in horror, the monkey got electrocuted and fell to the ground. The moment this happened, the hungry dog quickly picked up the monkey in its mouth and took off. Reuben became enraged and hastily ran after the dog.

While chasing the dog through the narrow streets, he picked up a stone and threw it with all his might at the animal, striking it on the neck. Immediately, the dog released the monkey and ran down the alley. Sadly, Reuben discovered that his monkey had died, and filled with emotion, he began to weep. As I tried to console him, he lamented, claiming how faithful this monkey had been to him. Seeing Reuben stricken with grief, I told him to go home, and that Sarah and I would return the following day to see him. Surprisingly, as we were about to leave, we were startled to see the owner of the jewelry stall and two policemen hurrying towards Reuben. As they approached him, the owner began accusing Reuben of sending his monkey to steal a necklace from his showcase. Sarah and I immediately refuted his claim, but when the police saw the two of us were homeless people, they simply ignored us, arrested Reuben and took him into custody.

This unfortunate incident distressed Sarah and me, as it was sad to see Reuben charged for a crime he hadn't committed. When Sarah saw Reuben being taken away by police, she blamed herself for being inconsiderate, realizing that she had never stopped for a moment to think how such a poor lad could afford to buy her an expensive necklace. For several days Sarah and I kept on agonizing over what we could have done to prevent such an unfortunate thing from happening.

CHAPTER 3

Seven weeks later we all got a surprise visit from Lucifer. He stood approximately twenty meters from us, joyfully waving his hands. As Lucifer slowly stepped forward, he gave a joyous shout, "I have eight hundred dollars, and I want to share it with you!" The five of us did not want to take any chances with this cunning man, so we began to gather up stones to throw at him. Seeing this, Lucifer quickly pushed his hand into his pocket, took out a handful of notes and began waving them at us. When Julius saw the money, he became excited and immediately invited Lucifer to join us. However, the rest of us did not trust him and made it clear that we were not going to allow him to join our group unless he told us from whom he got the money.

Seeing how determined we were to know the truth, Lucifer politely asked if he could come a little closer to talk to us. Allowing him to do so, we were all taken aback when he explained that after he had departed from us, he secretly went into the tent of a homeless man and stole some of his clothing. Dressed in the man's attire, he went into the central part of the city and robbed an elderly woman who had just come out of a bank with a fair amount of cash. Lucifer, seeing us looking shocked by what he said, pleaded with us not to tell anyone about the crime he had committed. To entice us, Lucifer offered each of us one hundred dollars. When Amelda saw the money, her eyes opened wide and in a flash she plucked it out of Lucifer's hand. She looked pleased and told Lucifer not to worry, for she would remain quiet about the robbery. Within seconds Sarah and Julius said the same. However, Sebastian and I flatly refused his money. Both of us had similar thoughts about Lucifer, that he was a lazy man who was determined to bully or rob others to survive.

When Amelda heard Sebastian and me refuse the money Lucifer had stolen, she looked disappointed. In a soft tone she said, "We are all poor, and this money will give us plenty of joy in this short life." I pointed out that while she was feasting on the money Lucifer stole, the elderly woman who had been robbed would be lamenting over the loss of her savings. Amelda, still determined to persuade me, begged me not to agonize over this, claiming the elderly woman must be wealthy because of the large sum of money she had, and that her sorrows would not last forever.

Seeing the worried look on their faces, I became sympathetic and promised that I would remain silent only if they took an oath not to support Lucifer in such a sinful act again. Immediately, the four of them agreed and quickly thanked me. In a joyous mood, Amelda called on all of us to celebrate what she considered the happiest day of her life. Emotionally stirred, she hurried into her tent and brought out two bottles of strong liquor to share with everyone. On this occasion, Sebastian and I did not join in their celebration, since we weren't pleased with what they were doing. We both harbored similar beliefs that it is better to beg than to steal from others. Soon it was party time and Amelda, Sarah, Lucifer and Julius began to sing and dance. Their feasting went on for several hours until they became drunk from the inordinate amount of liquor, and went to bed early that night.

On the following day, Lucifer woke up early and left for the city while the rest of us were still asleep. An hour later, he returned with a portable radio, two large pizzas and two bottles of liquor. In a happy mood he woke up Sarah, Amelda and Julius and told them to continue the party. Judging from how quickly they all came out of their places, it was clear that they were willing to enjoy themselves as long as possible. Minutes later, the feasting began and after a few drinks, Lucifer turned on the radio loud.

Soon, Sarah became drunk, climbed onto a bench and began a lewd form of dancing with Lucifer, while Amelda and Julius kept urging them on. As the party continued, Sebastian and I were in shock when we saw Sarah revealing parts of her body as she danced. Embarrassed by such indecent behavior, the two of us discussed what we could do to stop them. Sebastian soon decided to approach Amelda and ask her to stop the music and dancing, for the noise could attract the police to investigate what was taking place under the bridge. When Sebastian appealed to Amelda to stop the music, she became angry and shouted, "You are a pain in the ass!" What was even more disheartening was that Julius joined Amelda in condemning him. Sebastian, realizing that both of them were drunk, avoided a confrontation, and casually walked back to his place without saying anything.

Amid the celebrating, I was surprised by how much Julius' behavior towards Lucifer had changed. Now that Lucifer had money and seemed willing to share it, Julius was eager to do anything Lucifer requested. I became annoyed when Lucifer asked Julius to fetch him an extra slice of pizza, and he moved in such a hurry to get it that he almost stumbled over a log on the ground. But what really convinced me that Julius had become an "ass kisser" was when Lucifer's shoelaces became open while dancing and Julius knelt down to tie them.

By noon, Lucifer, Amelda, Sarah and Julius became so drunk that they staggered to their places. After this there was a long period of silence, for the four of them did not come out of their tents until the following day.

When they all awoke the next day, Lucifer gave Amelda and Sarah fifty dollars and told them to go out and purchase more food, alcohol and cigarettes. Receiving so much money once more, they both became excited and immediately left to purchase the items.

In days to follow, Sebastian and I discovered that Sarah and Lucifer were having an intimate relationship, for on a few occasions we saw them kissing. I was disappointed, as I could not comprehend how Sarah could have an affair with a man who was violent and cunning. Sebastian and I also took notice of the close friendship between Amelda, Julius and Lucifer, and how unfriendly they became to both of us.

On a day that abounded with sunshine, the four of them had been drinking heavily. In high spirits, Lucifer started to play his music and encouraged Sarah to dance for him. Being drunk, she started her lewd form of dancing once more. As Sarah continued dancing to one song after the other, Sebastian became annoyed and yelled at her to stop. He then made a serious threat, claiming that if the four of them did not stop their foolish behavior, he would report the stolen money to the police. Lucifer became concerned and immediately stopped the music. He then asked the others to halt the feasting. Speaking in a softer tone, Sebastian said to them that they were portraying a bad image of our fellow homeless people, as many might think of us as shameless. He then said that regardless of their status in life, they should not relinquish their duty to uphold moral behavior. Listening attentively to what Sebastian said, they all looked unhappy and slowly walked back to their places.

Over the next couple of days, Lucifer continued to buy food and alcohol for Sarah, Amelda and Julius; however, they appeared a little more discreet in that they no longer played any music or danced. Sadly, all the fun and feasting they were having ended when Lucifer soon ran out of money. Now that Lucifer was totally broke, it was unbelievable to see how quickly he lost all his friends. Amelda, Sarah and Julius totally disowned him and returned to their daily task of begging in the streets. Lucifer was now downcast, as he could not believe that his friends would abandon him so quickly. Seeing him in a state of despair, it was difficult for Sebastian and me to tell what was filtering through his mind.

From the wild spending and sharing of the money Lucifer had stolen, Sarah and Amelda profited the most, for whatever money he gave them they hid most of it. Unfortunately, when he later begged them to lend him some money, they refused, claiming that they had spent it all. What was even more disheartening was that Julius, who was so attentive to Lucifer before, shunned him, also claiming that he had no more money.

Seeing Lucifer so unhappy, I became sympathetic and gave him four dollars and an old oversized shirt that I had. What happened immediately after this was memorable, as Lucifer got down on his knees and thanked me. With a gentle smile, he turned to me and said that some day he would repay me in a manner that I would never forget. Then he politely asked me if I could lend him the yarmulke that I wore. Believing that he no longer harbored any ill feelings for me, I went into my tent and gave him another one that I had.

The following day, wearing the shirt and the cap I had given him, Lucifer told me that he was going to the city to beg and would return later. I was drawn to think that he had become a changed man, probably learning a lesson from all the silly things he had done.

Two hours later, Lucifer returned and immediately went straight into his tent. Within minutes he was out and dressed in the old outfit that he had worn before. He then returned the yarmulke and clothing that I gave him and told me that they were uncomfortable and he desperately needed to change them. As I held the clothing, wondering what to do with them, I saw a few policemen and a couple of trained dogs hurrying towards us. As the dogs were barking continuously, Sarah, Amelda, Sebastian and Julius ran out of their places to see what was happening. At this point I honestly felt the police were coming to force us out from this secluded area. However, this was not the case, for the two dogs pounced on Lucifer and pulled him to the ground. Immediately, the police handcuffed Lucifer and began questioning him. Lucifer admitted that he had robbed another elderly woman, leaving Sebastian and me in shock.

After Lucifer was charged, he was escorted by police out of the area. As I stood in awe at what had happened, one of the officers approached me and took the yarmulke and shirt out of my hand, claiming that he needed them as evidence. I immediately realized that Lucifer had deceived me by using my belongings to commit the robbery, hoping that I would be accused of it.

Analyzing this incident, I came to realize that Lucifer was ungrateful, for in spite of all the effort I made to help him, he was determined to discredit me. While Sebastian was still reflecting on what Lucifer had done, I politely asked if he could explain why such a man would not relinquish his hatred for me. Sebastian explained that an arrogant person like Lucifer does not like to be told that he is at fault, and my disapproval of his wrongdoings would always agitate him. He said that I was too naïve when Lucifer grinned and promised that he would repay me in a manner that I would never forget. Sebastian claimed that Lucifer was being sarcastic, and that I should never put my entire trust in someone who speaks with sarcasm, for it is difficult to tell what their sincere feelings are. Sebastian further said that what was preventing me from becoming vindictive toward Lucifer might be that I was an educated or caring person who tended to worry about the consequences of my actions. As a result, I would be inclined to settle my disputes with others through gentle persuasion or meaningful dialogue.

Two days later, we were all astonished when a few policemen came under the bridge to order us to pack all our belongings and leave the area. One of the officers claimed that people in the neighborhood were complaining about us being noisy, and our presence devaluing their property.

It was a disappointing moment for Sarah, Julius, Amelda and me, since our earlier disputes over the stolen money and the feasting left us divided. Not wanting to be forced out by the police, I asked Sebastian to follow me and we would seek elsewhere to live. He was my closest friend, and willingly he joined me in packing up our belongings to leave. As we did this, Sarah and Amelda began to argue with the police about being given such short notice to leave. In spite of what they had to say, they had to abide by the law, and in the end, they too dismantled their tent to leave.

The days to follow became a difficult period for Sebastian and me, for we had no fixed home, and to avoid being harassed by police, we slept in the dark corners of alleys and at the back of old condemned buildings. It was frightening there, for on some occasions there were incidents of shootings, as those involved in drug trafficking often came to such areas to make secret deals. Some nights there were occasional quarrels among other homeless people, who argued over space and the contents they found in people's garbage.

With no specific place to rest, Sebastian and I often ended up not seeing each other for days. We were also separated at times because we collectively decided not to beg in close proximity, since we found it more lucrative in separate areas. Because of the great distances we had to cover on some occasions, we found it less tiring to spend a couple of nights in an area before moving to another.

As Sebastian and I continued to beg in various parts of Beaverton, now and again we found it distressing to cope with insults from some people who yelled at us to go elsewhere. Though we were occasionally snubbed, Sebastian and I saw no reason to hate such people. As beggars, it was important that we remain polite because our survival depended on the handouts from people.

CHAPTER 4

Eight months later, while walking alone on a busy city street, I saw Sarah and her mother Amelda sitting on a public bench looking relaxed. Believing that they were still angry with me, I was reluctant to approach them. However, since I had known them for some time, and for the greater part they were kind to me, I decided to rekindle my friendship with them. As I got closer to find out how they were keeping, I was astonished to see Sarah pregnant. When Amelda cast her eyes on me, she was ecstatic, for she gave me a big hug and then happily said to me that she and Sarah had been searching several months for me. As I was about to say how happy I felt to meet them again, Amelda left me in awe when she claimed that Sarah was pregnant by me, and she would be giving birth any day now. Knowing that I had not shared the same bed with Sarah, I found it difficult to comprehend why Amelda was saying that I was going to be a father.

Seeing Sarah with a tired and gloomy look, I honestly felt it was not the right time to confront her about this matter. Turning to Amelda, I immediately advised her to take Sarah to the Sinai shelter to get help. However, Amelda objected, claiming that when Sarah was ready to give birth, she would be the one delivering the baby. Knowing Amelda's troubled state of mind, I was disappointed by this. As I pondered what to say, she began pleading with me to accompany them home because Sarah needed my help during these final days of her pregnancy. Feeling sorry about their mental illnesses and how they were going to take care of the infant, I decided to follow them home. Not saying anything to disappoint Amelda, I allowed her to assume that I was the father of the child Sarah was bearing.

As Amelda walked ahead of us, I took the opportunity to walk abreast with Sarah who looked dejected. I then quietly asked her by whom she was pregnant. Sarah quietly replied, "Lucifer!" She then asked me to keep it a secret because her mother had always wanted me to be her son-in-law, and she had repeatedly told her mother that I was the father of the child. I felt relieved that Sarah was speaking the truth.

As Sarah and I continued to walk abreast, she quietly told me that from the moment she found out that she was pregnant, she became unhappy. It suddenly dawned on her that the child she was bearing was a product of the most sinful man she had ever met. She dolefully admitted that she deeply regretted having an affair with Lucifer and wished she could die before giving birth. A distraught Sarah believed the child she was going to bear would constantly remind her of Lucifer's bad deeds.

What Sarah said left me speechless, as I could not gather my thoughts quickly enough to comment on her unhappiness. Not sure about what to say, I decided to change our conversation by asking Sarah to ignore her mother and go to the Sinai shelter where they could make arrangements for her to get medical help. Unfortunately, because of Sarah's mental condition, I could not convince her, for she kept on telling me that her mother was capable of delivering a child.

Finally, after twenty minutes of walking, we arrived at a used car dumpsite that had been abandoned for years. Here, Amelda pointed to an old abandoned car and told me it was their home. I was astonished, as I was expecting them to take me to a makeshift tent. However, when considering how difficult it was for a homeless person to find a place to rest, I quickly became composed and accepted their humble home. Amelda, who had already occupied the driver's seat, told me to sit next to her, and to let Sarah sit alone in the back, since she needed the extra space to lie down. Amelda spent most of the time talking about what a proud grandmother she was going to be when Sarah gave birth. After listening to her constant prattling for almost an hour, Sarah and I eventually became bored and fell asleep.

A few hours later, Sarah appeared restless as she kept tossing and turning in her sleep. I realized how uncomfortable it was for her to sleep in the abandoned car. Slowly, Sarah's movement increased and she started to moan. Softly she said, "Rabbi, I am going to give birth any moment now." I immediately shook Amelda, who had fallen asleep, to tell her what Sarah had said. Surprisingly, Amelda told me not to worry because she was going to drive Sarah to a hospital. Like someone who had gone completely out of their mind, she began mimicking the starting of a motor vehicle, and started turning the steering wheel wildly, imitating a car being driven at high speed. Because of Amelda's mental condition, I instantly realized the onus was on me to deliver the infant.

Amid all the excitement, as I urged Sarah to push in order to hasten giving birth, Amelda kept telling me not to panic because we would soon be arriving at the hospital. Suddenly,

I felt the head of the newborn in my hand and carefully I proceeded with the task of delivering the infant.

From the moment the newborn cried, Amelda instantly stopped pretending to drive the car, and on her face I saw tears of joy. When Amelda saw the infant was a baby boy, there was a sudden transformation in her behavior, for she no longer acted crazy. She hurriedly came out of the car and quickly took out some used clothing from the trunk to wrap the infant. With the child adequately covered in a blanket, Amelda carefully gave the infant to me to hold, proudly saying, "Here is your son." Sarah, seeing how happy her mother looked when she said this, chose to remain silent. Though I was not the father of this child, holding the infant in my hands made me feel as if it were my own. Amid our joy, Sarah lay quietly after giving birth. However, as I held her hand to comfort her, I felt that it was very warm, leading me to believe that she had developed a fever. Unfortunately, her fever lasted through the night and I could not pause to rest. As she lay ill with droplets of perspiration trickling down her forehead, she managed a faint smile and then gently reached out to touch my hand without speaking. It was difficult to tell what was filtering through her mind; I could only guess that it was an affectionate way of thanking me for delivering her child. While Amelda and I remained watchful of Sarah in the wee hours of the night, the newborn infant appeared restless and often cried. As Sarah's illness seemingly worsened, I prayed earnestly for the break of dawn so that I could seek help for both mother and child.

Early the next morning, I hurried to a nearby shop to buy milk for the infant because Sarah was too weak to breast-feed him. Returning, I gave Amelda the milk to feed the child. As I was about to rush out once more to seek medical help for Sarah, Amelda, holding the infant with one hand, reached out with the other and grabbed my trousers, tearfully begging me not to leave. On her face she had a look of despair, as if to say her daughter might soon pass away. At that point I could not afford to spend any time comforting her because Sarah was gravely ill. Without uttering a word to Amelda, I quickly withdrew from her and headed to the Sinai shelter to seek help.

Surprisingly, when I got to Sinai and began explaining to the guard at the main entrance that a woman had given birth in a car located on a dumpsite, he did not believe my story and told me to seek help elsewhere. I could only guess that by seeing me so poorly clad, he assumed I was a homeless man with a mental illness who was fabricating a story to get some attention. Desperately pondering on what to do next, I realized that I had to get the police involved. Not wanting to meet them, I used a public phone to inform them about the matter. Then it suddenly dawned on me that instead of going to Sinai, I should have notified the police without delay, since it was probably the best way to get emergency help.

Arriving twenty minutes later at the place where I had left Sarah, I was surprised to see how quickly the police and paramedics had arrived at the scene. As I stood aloof watching in despair, I learned from another homeless man that Sarah had died and the police were investigating the matter. Since I had escaped from a mental asylum, I realized that I had to distance myself from this tragic incident, as any police involvement could lead to me being sent back to a mental institution. In the end, it distressed me to see Amelda and the baby being taken into police custody.

For the next few days I slept in various parts of the ghetto. I continued to lament over Sarah's death and about the future of Amelda and the infant. However, concerned that Amelda was homeless and about the safety of the newborn child,

I was drawn to think the child would be better protected under the law.

A week later I decided to go searching for a more lasting place to dwell, since it was becoming too stressful to sleep in different places at night. Being concerned about the safety of some areas, I desired to find a place that was more peaceful.

One day, after having walked approximately three miles, I saw an old abandoned railway station and decided to go underneath it to see if it was livable. Looking cautiously around I saw no one. However, as I advanced further, I detected a strong scent of marijuana. Thinking that there might be drug dealers in the vicinity, I felt a bit uneasy and slowly I took a few steps back. But I inadvertently bumped into a little person, dressed in white clothing with a shabby yellow scarf hanging from his neck. As my heart pounded from fright, I was astonished when I turned around and discovered the man was Alvis. Amid this surprise we were both delighted to see each other. Alvis, still sounding proud, claimed that he was expecting me, and on the same note, he said that a second person would come to visit and the two of us would become his disciples. Looking at me with a delighted smile, Alvis said, "Today is the happiest day of my life. I've been waiting almost two years for you to come and visit me." Outlandishly dressed, he pranced around like a proud peacock, then stopped suddenly and pointed to an old mattress, saying it was my bed. After that, he showed me another bed which he claimed would be for his second disciple. Alvis' weird behavior and the silly things he said drew me to think that he was not mentally sound.

Shortly after, Alvis reached into a box beside him and took out a solid slab of cheese. Using a knife with a broken tip, he cut a few slices from it and offered them to me. Feeling hungry, I gladly accepted the cheese and expressed my gratitude. Considering that Alvis was happy to see me, and offered me a bed and food, I came to think that apart from his strange behavior, he showed that he was generous.

Seeing Alvis dressed in white, having long hair and claiming to be wise, I was led to believe that he had joined some religious sect. While I tried to figure out what Alvis was getting at when claiming that I would become his disciple, he asked me to follow him into an area where he had a few pieces of furniture. There, he climbed into a high chair and told me to sit on the ground.

Observing me from his chair, Alvis said that he had something confidential to tell me. Believing that it might be important, I moved a little closer to hear him. I was puzzled when he claimed that he was the 112th descendant in the ancestral line of the Great King Solomon of the biblical period. He also said that in all, two men would come to visit him, and one would die while the other would inherit all his wealth. Alvis then gloomily said that he was going to die on the 21st of May, which was approximately two months away, and the one who was going to inherit his wealth must be by his side on that day. I became momentarily speechless and in shock when Alvis suddenly opened another box, took out a needle and injected himself with cocaine. As I watched in awe, he further baffled me when he reached into the same box and took out a joint of marijuana and began to smoke it.

Seeing me astonished at what he was doing, Alvis then offered me the drug to inhale, but I politely refused, telling him that I did not smoke. Shortly after, Alvis became dazed from the drug, and slowly he climbed down from his chair and bypassed me to sit on his bed. Minutes later, he fell into a trance and, before I could say anything to him, he passed out.

While Alvis remained sedated, I began deliberating whether or not to share the same place with him. However, when thinking about the various places I had lived before, this one was much more peaceful, and above all it had a solid roof to shelter me when it rained. Though Alvis' behavior was unusual, he was not a harmful person. From the few hours I spent with him, I discovered him to be the generous type, for he seemed willing to share whatever little he had. Taking into consideration that he was not argumentative or hurtful, I made my mind up to stay in the same place with him. With Alvis still sound asleep, I decided to rest on the bed he had offered me, as the journey to this abandoned railway station had been long and tiring.

The next day, when Alvis appeared in a better frame of mind, I asked what he had done after the incident in which he was mistreated by Julius and Lucifer. Alvis explained that he went in search of a new home, and found this old abandoned railway station suitable for living. When he first arrived here, the only creature present was a goat that came each night to rest under the station. He did not scare the animal away, and as the goat became accustomed to his presence, he treated it like a pet. Showing fondness for the animal, he soon began to take milk from its udder, and to this day he still got fresh milk from the goat.

Looking anxiously around, I could not see any trace of the animal, so I questioned him as to where he kept it. Alvis replied that when he shared the same space with the goat, the place began to smell awful with its feces. As a result, he had to take the animal to a place that was not too far away. Curious to see where he kept the animal, I asked him to take me there. Alvis walked me to an area where there was tall, lush, green grass. In the middle of it, the goat, which was as white as snow, was tied to a stick that was firmly planted in the ground. Alvis then surprised me when he mentioned that one day he was going to kill the goat and offer it as sacrifice to God. But I simply ignored him, believing the years of drug abuse must have affected his mind.

Since Alvis lived approximately three miles from the central part of the city, I decided to stay with him for a few days to see if it was worthwhile begging in the surrounding area. Unfortunately, after two days, I realized the area where he lived was too sparsely populated, as I had to spend hours begging before someone would offer me a little money. The only thing that was encouraging me to stay was that Alvis treated me with kindness, for on each of these days, he offered me a small glass of goat's milk and some of the biscuits he had saved in a jar. This, however, was not enough for me to survive on, so after three days with him, I decided to go to the central part of the city to beg.

Arriving in the city area after a tiresome walk, I noticed a large number of people leaving the area with some of their belongings. I was puzzled by this, and it was not until I received orders from a policeman to leave immediately that I became aware that the area was going to be hit by a hurricane. The officer claimed that everyone had been informed three days ago to leave and he could not understand why I was still present in the area.

As I walked away from the officer pondering what to do, I observed that while the majority of people were leaving with their families, others chose not to do so as they were adamant about not leaving their homes. Seeing a small group of homeless people, I inquired where they were going to seek shelter from the hurricane. I found out that the majority of homeless people in the surrounding area had gone to the Sinai shelter, but this group that I met for the first time claimed that they would not be going to Sinai, because they did not believe that a severe storm was coming. However, a short while later, the place appeared a little darker, and believing that it would soon rain, they collectively agreed to go into an old abandoned two-storied building to seek shelter. Not wanting to be left alone or caught in a severe storm, I decided to join them.

Inside the building, we all felt that it was safer to remain on the first floor, as the stairs leading up to the second floor were badly decayed and not safe to climb. As I cautiously walked around to view a couple of rooms, my sudden presence scared away many bats, which quickly flew through openings in the walls and broken windows. Fearing that one of us might inadvertently step on a part of the flooring that was weak, I told the others it would be safer for us to remain in the hallway.

Approximately an hour later, the place became much darker, and I began to hear the whooshing sound of the wind. Soon, the wind gathered momentum and amid it came a torrential downpour of rain. As we all sat quietly on the first floor of the building, we suddenly became scared when the entire building started to vibrate from being encircled by the wind. Amid it all, the windows and doors rattled noisily, creating an eerie sound that was irritating at times.

This day proved to be a frightful one, as the storm turned out to be more severe than we had expected. Because the roof of the building was old and the windows got shattered by the heavy winds, we became totally drenched from the rain. Amid this horrifying experience, we were struck several times by particles of glass and wood which came off the shattered windows. To avoid being hit by scattered debris, we occasionally moved from one room to the next as the direction of the wind varied.

This severe storm lasted for approximately ten hours, and by midnight it had fully ended. At that time there was total silence as no one came out of their homes. For the rest of this dark and dreary night with ghostly clouds looming above, we all sat in our wet clothing silently praying for the break of dawn.

Early the following morning, our homeless group decided to leave the building to witness the damage caused by the hurricane. Surprisingly, when we came out we were all left in awe to see hundreds of people smashing the windows of unattended stores to steal clothing, jewelry and various merchandise. It was the first time I had seen people behave so violently, as some even broke into a store that sold guns and knives. Judging from the expensive merchandise people were running off with, food seemed of little importance. Witnessing the looting, it dawned on me why some people were so adamant about not leaving the area prior to the hurricane. It was disheartening that while many people tried to help some who were injured, others seemed not to care, as they kept smashing the windows of stores to steal.

The place looked totally ravaged. Apart from the wreckage of homes, light poles and trees, most of the streets were covered in approximately two feet of water. As our homeless group stood watching the riotous crowd, we saw a large number of fruits and vegetables floating on top of the water. They were from the stalls of sellers who had to leave most of their produce behind just prior to the hurricane. As some of the fruits floated by, a few from our group began to take them from the water to eat. Taking into consideration that no homeless persons were taking part in the riot or stealing made me realize the homeless were not the lowest class of citizens. It was clear to me that those who were involved in theft were the lowest class, since stealing was more important to them than helping those who were injured and in desperate need of help.

Later in the day, when hundreds of police and volunteers arrived in the disaster area, the rioting suddenly came to a halt as police began to arrest many who were running off with stolen merchandise. Witnessing the valiant efforts of volunteers and police, who began scouring ravaged homes to help people while having to deal with looters and angry mobs, made me realize how caring some people were in these circumstances. The hurricane was an act of nature, and while some people complained about not getting enough help, I as a homeless person had nothing to argue or complain about since I had no worldly possessions.

Soon, with the help of police and volunteers, the homeless group and I were sent to a huge government facility that was set up as a temporary shelter. Here, I found people of various statuses, and it was surprising to our homeless group that no one treated us with disrespect. With everyone in the shelter temporarily homeless, we were all in a similar predicament. It was hard to believe that many who would have otherwise shunned us prior to the hurricane now had to stay with us under the same roof, and even to eat with us at the same table.

A week later when most of the water had subsided, people were allowed to enter and leave the city freely. After having spent a week at the temporary shelter, I decided to return to the place where Alvis lived, hoping the damage by the hurricane might be less there. Fortunately, because the railway station was located on high land, the damage from water was far less than in the city.

Alvis was happy to see me, for he kept telling me that he was so concerned about my safety during the storm that he could not rest peacefully at night. It was pleasing to hear him express his concern, as it made me feel that he was a loyal friend.

*   *   *   *   *

Two weeks later, I decided to go to the central part of the city to look for my old pal Sebastian, to learn how he had made out during the storm, and also to let him know about my new home. Unfortunately, my search for him became hectic, for no matter where I went in the city streets and alleys, I could not find him. In the end, it took me almost six hours before I saw him coming out of a store with his left arm wrapped in bandages. My thoughts shifted from the storm, and I immediately began questioning him about the dressing.

Sebastian told me that two days before, he was stabbed in his arm when trying to stop a fight between Julius and the owner of a food store. While walking one day, he saw Julius drunk and arguing with the storeowner, who wanted him to move from the front of his shop and beg elsewhere. The owner claimed that Julius was annoying his customers by begging them for money as they entered his store. When Julius refused to leave, the storeowner pushed him and immediately a fight broke out. During the melee, the owner went back into his shop and brought out a knife, and began wielding it at Julius. Upon seeing this, Sebastian intervened to settle their dispute, and in the process, he got cut on his left arm while Julius received two serious stab wounds in his abdomen. Sebastian went on to say that when the police arrived, the owner of the store was arrested while he and Julius were rushed to the hospital.

When I asked Sebastian whether he had seen Julius since then, he looked at me sorrowfully and said that Julius died on his way to the hospital. I became deeply saddened when I heard this, for it was a cruel way for a homeless man with few friends to die.

Believing that at some point in time Sebastian might inquire about Sarah and Amelda, I decided not to keep Sarah's untimely death a secret, so I recounted her sad story, which also involved Amelda and the infant. Sebastian was dismayed, for Sarah was just thirty-four years of age when she died. It took some time for us to be composed after each of us had learned of the death of people we had spent years with.

Since Sebastian was now seventy-six years of age and suffered from shortness of breath, I honestly felt that he needed the support of someone. He moved much slower than before and had a tired look. By this time one would have expected him to quit the habit of smoking, but now and again, he would reach into his pocket to take out a cigarette. Feeling sympathetic, I began to encourage him to live with me below the railway station that I had recently discovered. Sebastian easily agreed, since he was not comfortable sleeping in dark alleys and at the back of old condemned buildings where rival gangs often got into fights.

Through my acquaintance with Sebastian over the years, I discovered him to be the type of person who could easily win friends, because of his amicable disposition. He always avoided a confrontation with people who were argumentative, since he believed in dialogue and preferred to reason with them. Believing that he had a sound educational background, I decided now to question him about his past. However, when I brought up this subject again, he was reluctant to talk about it and repeatedly shook his head to say no. Concluding that what he had in mind might be personal, I decided not to coerce him into telling me about it.

On our journey to the new place where I stayed, I had to make several stops to allow Sebastian to rest because of the shortness of breath he often experienced. It was during one of these stops that I saw a Jewish synagogue which I had passed several times before. On this occasion I developed a sentimental urge to attend this place of worship, for I had never visited one in almost eight years.

Thinking that Sebastian might be a religious person, I invited him to go with me to the synagogue to hear something inspirational. Surprisingly, Sebastian shook his head to say no, and with a gentle touch on my shoulder, he signaled me to go alone. From his subtle response it dawned on me that he might be of a different faith, so I affectionately asked him what his religion was. Again I was surprised when Sebastian replied that he did not belong to a specific faith. He said that he might be considered an atheist because his concept of God was different from the majority of religious followers. In his view, God is not a man who rules the world. Instead, he viewed the immeasurable universe to be a manifestation of God in which all are driven to perform actions for their survival.

Knowing that Sebastian was a soft-spoken man with moral concerns, I found it difficult to comprehend why he did not worship God. Still in doubt, I told him there must be something that he believed in, or perhaps he had some moral principles that he adhered to. Sebastian replied that there was no God that could help or protect him. He claimed that he was a secular humanist, meaning that he had his own moral beliefs which promote human goodness, but he did not belong to a specific faith. He further said that he could achieve a lot without the help of God or any supernatural power. I asked him, if this was so, why he chose to remain a beggar and not uplift himself in life. Pondering on what to say, he looked at me and said that he had made one serious mistake in his life which hindered him from achieving certain goals, and perhaps what he had to say might help to shape my life. Sebastian said that in his early years of adulthood, he had studied the origin and development of all major religions and earned a job as a lecturer on theology. Analyzing most of what he had studied, he came to conclude that all religious teachings which people claim to be the word of God are not so; instead they are a blend of primitive beliefs, rituals, ancient myths, history, and the beliefs and ideas of men who were considered wise. Sebastian claimed that by holding steadfast to such beliefs, people not only treated certain religious tenets with reverence but, looked toward a Savior for salvation. And while religion has comforted millions in times of misfortune, others who are adamant about their beliefs have silently harbored in their minds that their faith is the best.

Sebastian pointed out that though his beliefs were different from others, he did not discourage people from believing in God. He said that with me having set religious beliefs, I would be in a state of denial if a learned person were to tell me about the origin and development of what I strongly believed in. Sebastian claimed that the pleasing feeling human beings get from religion is associated with prayers, rituals, moral beliefs, and the festivities associated with various traditions and culture. He went on to say that the sorrows which emerge from religion come from the disputes between people of various faiths who adamantly believe the stories they are told by intelligent authors, and the teachings of wise men are the words of God. Sebastian claimed that religion is based more on beliefs than facts, hence the purpose of life would primarily remain a subject of conjecture and debate. He said that no one holds a monopoly on religion, as it is knowledge that was intended to be shared but not to stake one's life on when considering the impermanence of things. Sebastian indicated that though he was homeless and suffered a great deal, he was pleased with life on Earth for he had fulfilled his desire to study the scriptures of different faiths. And by selecting what was intelligible from each of them, he had developed a set of beliefs which made him a caring person.

Having listened attentively to what Sebastian had to say, I affectionately said to him that since he did not worship God, I was drawn to think that he was a sinner, and whenever I visited the synagogue, I would always pray that the Lord would forgive him. Sebastian said not to pray for him, but that I should pray for the millions who condemn others, quarrel over religion and pretend to be good. He said he had selected the best of various faiths and had incorporated them with his own beliefs. And as a result of this, he considered himself to be partly Zoroastrian, Hindu, Buddhist, Muslim, Christian and Jewish; therefore, he had no reason to quarrel with others over religion or harbor prejudiced feelings for anyone. Sebastian said that on a few occasions when he criticized some for the wrong they did to others, many called him racist, but this was not the case, for in his heart he sought to uphold what was fair and just.

After Sebastian's talk of tolerance, I asked him why, if he was so tolerant, he refused to go with me to the synagogue. In reply, he said that he did not despise my faith or hold an allegiance to any specific religion. He emphasized that, apart from the respect he had for others' faith, he was most supportive of what others believed in at the time of death, because prayers and comforting words not only soothe the minds of those who are stricken with grief, but they remain an integral part of the process of putting a closure to one's life on Earth.

What Sebastian had to say was not enough to convince me, as I had faith in God. Bearing in mind that he was old, I interrupted him at this point by asking, since he was not a religious person, how he would like his body to be disposed of when he died. Thinking that I might puzzle him with this question, I was surprised when Sebastian told me that considering he was a homeless man, I might either inform the police or take him to any place of religious worship where others could say prayers or pleasing words to comfort themselves. Sebastian indicated that whatever I or anyone did with his body after his death would not displease him, because his soul is a spark of the Almighty that is imperishable. He said that after the demise of one's body, the soul takes on another new human body in a cycle of birth, death and rebirth. Sebastian said that when we strive to uplift ourselves, it is our egotistic, or personality-self that we are seeking to improve, not the soul which is sinless. He claimed that with the discipline of understanding and the performance of acts of goodness, one's soul could merge with the Almighty after the demise of their physical body.

Continuing from where we had left off earlier, Sebastian went on to say that amid his years of success as a lecturer, he liked gambling on horses and playing poker. With time, he became a compulsive gambler and in the end he lost everything. Having squandered all his assets, his annoyed fiancée called off their wedding one week before the fixed date. Feeling embarrassed and dejected by what had happened, he turned to alcohol as a means of suppressing his sorrows. As a result of this, his relatives and friends shunned him. And in the end, he became a homeless person and joined others who lived on the streets. Sebastian added that over the years, these homeless people became his friends, and since then he had developed much affection for them.

Reflecting on his own life, Sebastian said that he was ashamed of his early mistakes in life, and deep within, he silently harbored the belief that he was a loser. Feeling discouraged since then, it never dawned on him to walk away from his homeless friends or to extricate himself from poverty. He said that when I asked him to come and live with me, he honestly felt that I should not waste my time taking care of him. He emphasized that I should not make the same mistakes or waste my youth as he did, for I still had the opportunity to better myself.

Downcast by his earlier failure, Sebastian said that he was old now, and did not have much energy to face new challenges in life. He then nervously opened the bag he usually carried around his shoulder, and reaching into it, took out a large amount of coins and single notes. Emotionally he said to me that he had saved it all in hope that one day he might be able to extricate himself from poverty, but unfortunately the meager sum took decades to save. He then offered me the money, saying that it amounted to three thousand and forty-two dollars. Sebastian claimed that he would not live much longer and that I should use this money to improve my status in life. Being offered that amount of money from a homeless man, while thinking about his struggles to save it, I found it difficult to accept. But after he repeatedly insisted that I accept the money, I eventually took it and expressed my gratitude.

After a long leisurely walk, Sebastian and I arrived at the place where Alvis lived. We were both astonished to see him sitting in a yogic posture with his eyes closed and a cigarette stuck in each ear. Seeing this man for the first time, dressed in white clothing, Sebastian looked bewildered. Leaning on my shoulder, he quietly asked in a whisper if Alvis was mentally ill. As the two of us cautiously walked around Alvis to see if he was awake, he slowly opened his eyes and welcomed Sebastian, saying, "You are my second disciple."

Once more, Alvis showed he was generous, for he offered us a piece of cheese and a bowl of water to drink. However, just as we began to feel a bit more comfortable with Alvis, he suddenly did the most bizarre thing I had ever seen. He gently took out the cigarettes from his ears and stuck one in his left nostril and the other in his mouth. He then lit both of them with a match and began inhaling the smoke. Both of us became speechless, as we could not say what he was up to. For a brief moment Sebastian placed his hands over his mouth and fixed his eyes on Alvis to see what he was going to do next. Seconds later Alvis started to cough, put out both cigarettes and threw them out of a small opening on the floor above us. Catching his breath, he cautioned both of us that he was going to die on the 21st of May, and one of us must be with him on that day to inherit all his wealth.

Witnessing the strange behavior of Alvis, Sebastian became reluctant to stay with him. He whispered in my ear that Alvis was weird and we should go elsewhere. After pondering, I quietly suggested to Sebastian to let us spend a few days with Alvis, and if we found him annoying, both of us would leave.

To encourage Sebastian to stay, I told him that our journey elsewhere would be long and it was too late now to go searching for another shelter. I then showed him the surrounding area of this place and pointed out its serenity. I must say that his eyebrows lifted up with what he saw, for it was scenic and peaceful, and with the flooring above, he was sure of one thing: he would never get wet when it rained.

Once Sebastian finally agreed to stay, I told Alvis that Sebastian was like a father to me and, being in poor health, he was going to need some support from us. From here on, I decided to do almost all the chores of buying food and tending to Sebastian, as it became a struggle for him to walk long distances.

A few days later, Alvis mentioned to Sebastian and me that he was going into a dense field about thirty meters away to fetch us a cup of goat's milk. Sebastian was puzzled when he heard this, for I had never mentioned to him that Alvis had a goat. When Alvis left, I took the opportunity to tell Sebastian that Lucifer had once humiliated Alvis, and when he first came to this place to live, he discovered a goat that came to rest each night under the station. I explained that with Alvis having almost no friends, his survival depended much on the milk from the goat that he now claimed to own.

When Alvis returned with the milk, both Sebastian and I were thankful, since it was something we seldom drank. Afterward, Alvis requested that Sebastian and I follow him to bear witness to him offering his goat as sacrifice to God. Sebastian became annoyed, and asked Alvis why he wanted to kill the animal that had been so faithful to him. Without any deliberation whatsoever, Alvis picked up the knife that he often sliced cheese with and told Sebastian and me to follow him. As Alvis was about to leave, Sebastian tried to persuade him by explaining that this belief he had was ancient, and to kill in the name of God was a sinful act. However, Sebastian got completely ignored, as Alvis hurriedly walked away from us with the knife in his hand. Concerned about what he intended to do, Sebastian and I decided to follow him.

When we got into the area where Alvis had the goat tied to a stick, we were both astonished to see him kneeling on the ground and praying with the knife clasped between his hands. Shortly after, Alvis got up and quickly pounced on the animal to wrestle it to the ground. However, since he was small, this proved to be a difficult task, as the goat began to jump wildly and eventually uprooted the stick that it was tied to. Petrified, the animal ran wildly through the bushes. In a desperate attempt to catch the goat, Alvis ran after it; however, he quickly ran out of breath and gave up the chase. As he walked back to us looking disappointed, Sebastian pointed out to him that he had made a serious mistake, because from this day on, he would no longer have any of the goat's milk.

In days to follow, Alvis slowly came to realize that he had made a serious mistake. Without the goat's milk, he now had to make more frequent visits to the Sinai shelter to get food, and this was something he tried to avoid because people at the shelter thought he was weird and often taunted him.

A week later, Sebastian became ill after contracting a serious flu. This soon developed into a terrible cough, making it difficult for him to breathe. He was so congested from the flu that time and again I could hear him wheezing heavily. Also making matters worse in this later stage of his life was the years of smoking now seemed to have adverse effects on his health. Being concerned about his physical condition, I told Alvis to keep an eye on Sebastian while I left to get some cough medicine for him.

Sadly, when I returned approximately thirty minutes later, I saw a team of paramedics and police taking away the partly covered body of Sebastian. Having faced a similar situation with Sarah's demise, I immediately assumed that Sebastian had died. However, to be absolutely sure I asked Alvis who appeared nervous and shaken, what had happened while I was away. He explained that after I had left, Sebastian began gasping for breath, and to get emergency help, he walked to a public phone and contacted the police. Alvis said that by the time he got back, Sebastian had passed away.

With Sebastian no longer alive, I became deeply saddened, for he was precious to me. He was a trusted friend whose encouraging words over the years had steadily reminded me to better myself and not to remain homeless forever.

*   *   *   *   *

After several weeks lamenting over Sebastian's death, I decided one day to visit the Jewish synagogue, as the feeling to embrace my Hebrew faith seemed stronger now than ever. As I was about to leave, Alvis assumed that I was going elsewhere to live. In spite of my telling him that I was not, he reminded me that if I were to do so, I must come back to visit him on the 21st of May because he was going to die on that day. Thinking that it meant a great deal to him, I made a promise to be with him on that day.

As I was about to depart, Alvis dolefully said that Sebastian and I were the two people he cared for the most, since we were the only ones thus far that had treated him with respect. He said that being a homeless little person, he was treated like an outcast by many who called him an ass, and because of this, he chose to live in isolation. Though he disliked going to Sinai, he still had to go there occasionally to get enough food to survive.

On my way to the synagogue, I visited the market place where Sarah and I had met Reuben, and while leisurely walking around, I got a pleasant surprise when I saw Reuben fetching a box of apples. As I anxiously called out his name, he put down the box and hurried to greet me. I observed that he had grown a little taller, and appeared less baby-faced, with few pimples and soft black hair on his face. As usual the clothing he wore all looked similar, for on the few occasions we met in the past, it was usually faded denim pants and an oversized, long-sleeved shirt.

I was surprised to see that Reuben had gotten another monkey to help him in taking the apples out of the box in preparation for sale. As I was about to tell Reuben how happy I felt to meet him, he anxiously looked around and asked, "Where is Sarah?" I was worried that I had to break the distressing news to him that Sarah had died. With him eagerly waiting, I felt that I had no other choice but to tell him that she had passed away.

The news of Sarah's untimely death immediately caused Reuben to become stricken with grief, as he lowered his head in total silence. I tried to comfort him by telling him that before Sarah had died, she always wanted to thank him for treating her with kindness. He was deeply touched and began to weep. Looking at me, he said that the first time he saw Sarah approaching his stall to buy apples, he became filled with pity when he saw that she was a homeless person. He went on to say that from this caring feeling, he instantly fell in love with her, and hoped that one day he would marry her and take her to the farm where he lived with his grandfather.

When Reuben mentioned whom he lived with, I felt confused, for judging from the shabby clothing Reuben wore, I honestly thought that he was homeless. Questioning him for the first time about where he was getting his supply of apples, I was surprised when he told me that he had trained his monkey to pick apples from the trees on his grandfather's farm. Reuben said that over the years he had saved a considerable amount of money from selling apples, and was hopeful that one day he would be able to buy more farmland.

Listening to Reuben impressed me, for he seemed to be an ambitious lad who appeared determined to uplift himself in life. Amid our chat, Reuben took me by surprise when he questioned me about my objective in life. I became defensive, as I could not believe that someone as young as Reuben would ask such a question. As I stood silently pondering what to say, Reuben again surprised me when he mentioned that he disliked people who were lazy. I could not comprehend what he was getting at; however, I was drawn to think that he was indirectly telling me that I should do something productive and not to remain homeless.

Knowing that Reuben was unaware of the hardships I had met, and probably had the wrong impression about me, I decided to tell him about some of the unfortunate things that had happened to me in life. Hearing me recount the experiences of losing my wife and children in a tragic fire, being discriminated against, and the years I spent in a mental institution, Reuben became sympathetic, telling me he now understood why I was homeless.

Having listened attentively to what I had to say, Reuben then explained that he had faced similar misfortunes, for at age eleven he lost both of his parents in a car crash, and in this accident, his right wrist got severed. Slowly pulling up the sleeves of his shirt, I was taken aback when I saw that he had no fingers on his right hand. Reuben indicated that after the tragic accident, his grandfather raised him on the farm. Sadly, he said that it compounded his problems when his grandfather had injured his back two years ago while picking apples, and since then he was left with the responsibility to take care of him. After his grandfather's injury, he had trained a couple of monkeys to pick the fruits on the farm so he could sell them. He went on to say that he chose not to beg because he did not think that he could cope with the stress of being homeless and being treated with contempt. Because of this, he would always remain resolute in his objective to become a prosperous farmer.

I became deeply touched by his sad story, since it reminded me that I was not the only one with problems. Reflecting on what Reuben said gave me a new outlook on life, since his determined effort to change his status in life made me want to do the same. In the end, my conversation with him was meaningful, for I was not only encouraged to uplift myself, but from that day on, Reuben became a loyal and trusted friend.

Arriving at the synagogue two hours later, I was fortunate to meet the rabbi named Albert Bernstein, who was standing at the main entrance to welcome the attendants. As he shook my hand and greeted me in a polite manner, I sensed he had an amicable disposition. When he began his sermon, I became entranced with what he had to say. His story of Joseph, the son of Jacob, reminded me much of what my mother once said to me about harboring never-ending hatred. It was good to learn from this biblical story about Joseph that even though he was sold into slavery by his brothers, Joseph still cared about them, for he brought his brothers and their families to Egypt.

After the sermon, I decided to have a private talk with Mr. Bernstein. Being homeless, I felt that someone like him would be compassionate and offer me help. Fortunately, he was sympathetic when I mentioned that I became homeless after having lost my wife and two children in a tragic fire. It turned out to be an exciting moment for me when the rabbi offered me a job as the caretaker of the synagogue, as well as a room to live in an adjacent building that was owned by the founders of the synagogue. In a joyful mood, I expressed my heartfelt thanks to the rabbi at a time when I desperately needed help to extricate myself from poverty.

With time, I grew to love this place of worship and considered it my home. Here, many worshippers who became my friends treated me with affection. It was confusing at times when people asked me my name and I spontaneously replied, "Rabbi," because my homeless friends had always addressed me by that name. When I impulsively said this, many churchgoers were respectful, for they seemed happy to meet me. I did not say this on purpose, but with my friends calling me Rabbi over the years, it took me a while to get everyone to know that Rabbi was my nickname and my correct name was Isaac.

One day, while performing my usual chores in the synagogue, I realized the date was the 21st of May, the day that I had promised to visit Alvis. Not wanting to disappoint him, I immediately left work and began my journey to the abandoned railway station.

Arriving at the place where Alvis lived, I detected the strong scent of marijuana. Cautiously approaching the area where Alvis usually sat, I was astonished to see him lying on his bed sedated. From his drowsy look I assumed that he had injected himself with cocaine. The moment Alvis saw me, he tearfully said, "I am going to die today, and I will be leaving all my wealth for you." Thinking that he was imagining things, I became puzzled when I saw him slowly pushing his hand under his pillow to take out a piece of paper that was neatly folded. He then gave it to me, saying that it was a winning lottery ticket, and it was a gift from him to me. Gently opening the paper, I saw that it was indeed a ticket but knowing his mental condition, I assumed it was not a winning one. I strongly believed that he was hopeful of winning money someday and freeing himself from poverty.

As the minutes went by, Alvis became sleepier, and soon he appeared lifeless. Thinking that he would eventually come out of his drowsy state, I decided to remain by his side. Unfortunately, Alvis never woke up, for an hour later when I tried to wake him, I discovered that he had silently passed away in his sleep.

Lowering my head in silence, I began deliberating what to do next since I could not leave his body to rot. Though

Alvis was a drug addict, I had respect for him after listening to how much he had suffered as an outcast. I could tell by his affection for Sebastian and me that he cared a great deal about those he considered sincere. This was the third time that I found myself in a helpless situation, ending up standing aloof from my homeless friends at the time of their demise. On this occasion, I realized that with Alvis apparently dying from a drug overdose, it would not be wise for me to remain at the scene, because I might have to undergo serious questioning by police. With this in mind I decided to leave, and then use a public phone to inform the police about his demise.

A week later it dawned on me that I still had the lottery ticket Alvis had given me in my wallet, and before I discarded it, I decided to go to a nearby store to see if it was a winning ticket. I suddenly became numb when the storeowner declared that I had won a million dollars. Gathering my thoughts amid an intense feeling of delight, I hurriedly took back the ticket from him, and an hour later I claimed the prize.

The following day, I told Mr. Bernstein that I had won a million dollars; however, I did not disclose that I had gotten it as a gift from someone else. He was pleased to hear this and wished me well in my endeavors to do something productive with it. He became even more elated when I told him that I would be donating half of it to create a mobile service that would provide a free meal to the homeless each day. When I also mentioned that I would be donating a portion of it to a public hospital in Beaverton and the rest to a program to help the homeless, he appeared puzzled by my generosity. I took the opportunity to say to him that this charitable act was something I had silently taken an oath to do, and now that I had gotten the money to do it, my desire was to fulfill that promise. Hearing this, Mr. Bernstein was delighted, and with his help, I was able to put my plans into effect.

CHAPTER 5

▼

Four years later, I had accomplished a great deal in life, as with the help of Mr. Bernstein and his friends, my plans to help the homeless were working out well. One day, while taking a leisurely walk, I met Amelda who had been begging in front of a nearby food store. With deep lines on her face, her hair gray, and the flesh on her arms sagging, she looked very old. As soon as Amelda saw me, she became elated and called out my pet name, Rabbi. Both of us were extremely happy to see each other, and like the reunion of a mother and her son, we began to talk about our current status and the important things that had happened after we became separated years ago. I learned that after Sarah had died, Amelda was put into a mental institution while her grandson was transferred to an orphanage. And it was only four weeks ago that she was declared medically sane and released from the asylum.

Listening to Amelda, I observed a complete change in her behavior, for she appeared in sober thoughts and spoke sensibly. She went on to say that she now lived at the Sinai shelter which she once had disliked. Amelda claimed that, being much older now, she felt it was better to live in the shelter and abide by their rules.

While observing how slowly Amelda moved, I noticed that her back was arched and she walked with a slight limp. Seeing her occasionally rubbing her back, I asked her if something was bothering her. She then said that over a year ago, she had developed a pain in her lower back and was diagnosed as suffering from osteoporosis by a doctor at the asylum. Amelda indicated that after she was taken into custody by police when Sarah had died, she had told them that her grandson's name was Joshua and his father was Jewish.

I instantly realized that deep in her heart she still sincerely believed that I was Joshua's legitimate father. When I asked Amelda when was the last time she saw Joshua, she happily exclaimed, "Yesterday!" To verify that what she said was true, I affectionately asked her to take me to see Joshua. Without hesitating, Amelda gladly agreed. She then said that I had to be patient with her, since she could not walk quickly because of her backache. I told Amelda not to worry because I'd get a taxi to take us there. But Amelda questioned where I was going to get the money to pay for a taxi. Seeing how concerned she was, I said to her that I worked at the synagogue and I was no longer homeless. But Amelda still did not believe what I said, and told me to show her how much money I had on me. It was not until I opened my wallet and showed her that I had eighty dollars that she agreed to travel by taxi.

On our journey, Amelda talked about how happy she felt that I was no longer a homeless person and how glad she was to have me as her son-in-law. She also expressed how distressingly painful it had been for her after Sarah had passed away. To this day, she still grieved for her daughter because she loved her dearly. In trying to comfort her, I told her that her grandson would one day grow up to take care of her.

As we continued our quiet chat, I was a little surprised when Amelda gently leaned towards me and plucked out a gray hair from my head, affectionately saying, "Rabbi, you are getting old." As she twirled this single strand of hair between her fingers, it dawned on me that some day I too would experience the problems of old age. While I was silently thinking about this, Amelda quietly said, "Rabbi, now that you are no longer homeless, what is it that you crave the most at this stage of your life?" I affectionately replied that the discipline of understanding was first on my mind, for as a man who was not perfect in my duty but loved God, it was my desire to dwell in unity with the Lord after my demise. In short, before I died on Earth, I would like to accomplish a fair level of sincerity, understanding and compassion to improve my personality-self. Amelda looked puzzled and declared that all of what I had said was foolish talk. She claimed that at this stage of my life, I should only wish for an abundance of wealth, since money wisely spent could help to improve the lives of many who were poor and homeless. It was at this point that our interesting talk came to an abrupt end when we reached our destination.

At the orphanage, I began to look pryingly at the boys to discern which one was Joshua. Amelda, seeing how curious I was, told me to follow her, since she knew where Joshua liked to play. With a broad smile on her face, she then led me to a room where I saw a group of boys his age. Suddenly, one of the boys came running towards her calling her Grandma. As the boy hugged Amelda and asked her for candies, I immediately realized that he was Joshua. Quietly, Amelda reached into her pocket and gave him a handful of sweets, before offering one each to the other boys.

Smiling happily, Amelda held Joshua in her arms and introduced him to me, telling him that I was his father.

Joshua, puzzled, looked at me for a brief moment and quickly continued chatting with his grandmother. Listening to him question Amelda about why she came so late to see him, and why she had so many of her teeth missing, I could tell he seemed curious and attached to his grandmother. Soon, Joshua went back to rejoin the group of boys he had been playing with, and both Amelda and I decided that it was time to leave.

On our way back, I decided to follow Amelda to the Sinai shelter, for I really wanted to continue my discussion with her. I took the opportunity to ask Amelda how Joshua became so attached to her. She explained that after she was declared medically sane, she immediately began inquiring from various government agencies about the whereabouts of her grandson. In the end, she found out that he was placed in this orphanage. After she brought candies for Joshua so regularly, he became familiar with her, and eventually she got him to call her Grandma.

Filled with compassion when thinking about Amelda's love and the effort she made to visit her grandson, I told her that from this day on, I would accompany her whenever she visited Joshua so he could get to know me. Amelda was happy when she heard this, since it was encouraging to her that I cared for Joshua. I honestly felt that if the young boy could accept me as his father, then it was possible that I could adopt him.

Reflecting on Amelda's earlier addiction to alcohol, I was curious to find out if she still drank alcohol, and was pleased when Amelda declared that she hadn't touched any alcohol in the past four years because it was prohibited at the asylum. She said that over the years she lost her craving for booze, and being without it so long, she discovered that she could think more clearly now.

In the coming months, Amelda and I made frequent visits to the orphanage to see Joshua. And on each occasion, she made a habit of telling him that I was his father. Amelda often pleaded with me to help get Joshua out of the orphanage, because she felt saddened saying goodbye to him after each visit. She claimed that with me having a permanent home, it would not be difficult to get him to live with me.

After months of frequent visits to the orphanage, Joshua eventually got to know me better and began calling me Daddy. This made me think that I had to keep this relationship with Joshua and Amelda a secret, believing that if Amelda told anyone that I was her son-in-law, this could complicate matters.

*   *   *   *   *

Sadly, six months later, Amelda passed away after developing a blood clot in her brain. This was a difficult period for me, for on each visit to the orphanage, Joshua asked, "How come Grandma doesn't come to see me anymore?" Even more distressing, Joshua wanted to know why I was leaving him at the orphanage and not taking him home with me. I now realized that I had to do something urgent to help this child who had become attached to me.

Days later, I met with Mr. Bernstein to tell him about the unfortunate story of Amelda and her grandson, and the promise I made to raise this boy as my son. I told the rabbi that I recently realized that I would not meet the sponsorship terms to adopt Joshua. I felt that if the representatives of the orphanage were to investigate my past and found out that I had been a mental patient, it was certain they would reject me. Though the rabbi was surprised about this, he was understanding and made a promise to help me.

The following day, Mr. Bernstein visited the orphanage to meet with some of its representatives to discuss the matter. He was an influential man who was well-respected in the community. However, in spite of his influence, it was not easy to gain their approval, since an investigation of my past showed that I had been a mental patient. Though Mr. Bernstein explained that I had this problem over a decade ago and I was now sane, the head of the orphanage indicated that it was imperative that I be checked out by a medical doctor to verify this matter. Fortunately, I was declared medically sane, and after months of negotiations, I was able to adopt Joshua as my son.

When a representative of the orphanage finally brought Joshua to my home, he came running towards me calling me Dad. This gave me a pleasant feeling, for I felt like a parent with an obligation to take care of him.

In the coming months I enrolled Joshua into a public school, as I honestly believed that a sound education would help him to think rationally. Since he was only six years old, I did not want to instill my religious beliefs in his mind at such a tender age, but allowed him to mature to an age where he could think more clearly, and perhaps be open-minded like Sebastian.

CHAPTER 6

▼

A decade later, I had grown much older, and during these years I was hopeful that Joshua would become a businessman when he reached adulthood. I honestly felt that creating employment was a way of giving minorities a start in life so that they could move on to a progressive path. Being once a homeless man, I came to realize how unkind this world could be to those who were poor and homeless.

Soon, Joshua became sixteen years of age, and I invited Mr. Bernstein, a few churchgoers and a couple of Joshua's closest friends to join in celebrating his sixteenth birthday. It was at this event that Joshua gave me a huge surprise when he declared, without consulting me, that he would be taking up studies to become a Jewish rabbi. Though I was disappointed when he said this, I tried my utmost not to show it. Rethinking matters, I came to realize that Joshua had made a personal choice and I should not discourage him from following the path of righteousness.

Raising my adopted son Joshua was a wonderful experience, for over the years, he proved to be kindhearted and helpful, always willing to help me in whatever household chores I had. Although he was the son of the most evil man I could think of, his noble qualities taught me that it is not because one is wicked or considered bad that means their offspring will be the same, and on the other hand, it is not because one is brought up by caring or religious parents that means one will turn out to be good. Thinking about this made me reflect on the biblical story of Ruth, and the family ancestral line of David and Jesus. In a contemplative mood, I also began to think about what Sebastian once said when he claimed that one's soul is a spark of an Infinite One, and each individual has a personality-self that is the subject of moral or immoral actions.

The next day, I returned to my daily tasks at the synagogue. Leaving the place of worship several hours later, I gazed at the sky and saw ominous rain clouds. Suddenly, there was a torrential downpour of rain, and to avoid getting thoroughly wet, I trotted to a nearby bus shed to seek shelter. Inside, I saw a homeless man sitting on the ground with his legs wide apart, asking for a drink of water. Looking carefully at this man, I was taken aback to see that he was Lucifer. Immediately, I introduced myself as Rabbi and he began to stare at me with astonishment. He seemed puzzled as he could not recognize me, being well-dressed and without my yarmulke at the time. It was not until I began to mention the names of old friends such as Amelda, Sarah and Julius that he came to realize who I was.

Looking at Lucifer sitting on the wet ground, I began deliberating what to do, since I had been repeatedly deceived by him in the past. However, since he had lost a considerable amount of weight and looked feeble, I felt that he was harmless. Seeing him so frail I became filled with pity, and I hurriedly ran out of the shed into the pouring rain to buy a bottle of water for him to drink. Returning with the water I quickly offered it to Lucifer, but I was taken by surprise that he would not lift his hands up to receive it. Quietly he said that he was seriously injured in the abdomen and needed me to pour the water into his mouth. I quickly knelt on the ground to examine his body and discovered the shirt he wore under an old jacket was soaked in blood. Shocked by what I saw, I gave him some of the water to drink and immediately I began to question him about his injury. I learned from Lucifer that only two days ago he was released from prison and today was the first day he came out to beg. He said that he had spent close to three hours begging and no one offered him any food or money. He came to this bus shed approximately an hour ago and saw a teenage boy waiting patiently for the bus. He began pleading with the youth to give him some money, but unfortunately, the teen claimed that he only had enough money to get onboard the bus. Feeling frustrated, he suddenly attacked the youth to rob him and was taken by surprise when the teenager pulled out a knife and stabbed him. The teen then ran away and since then he had been bleeding, mostly internally.

Fearing that he might die, I told him not to move, as I would rush out to seek help. Surprisingly, Lucifer begged me not to leave, saying, "I am afraid of dying and I want to make a confession." Tearfully, he said that of all the people he had met thus far, I was the only one who sincerely cared about him. It was only when he felt the blood on his abdomen and knew that he was going to die that he came to realize how compassionate I had been to him. Sorrowfully, he said that he could not believe that I was still willing to help him in spite of all the wrong he had done to me.

Lucifer went on to say that a short while before I came to the bus shed, he was distressed with the thought of dying and wanted to seek forgiveness from God. During that time, he constantly agonized over all the wrong he had done to me. And with this, he silently prayed to see me so that he could make amends and relinquish the hatred he had for me, because dying with hatred might stain his soul. He said when he got this feeling that he was going to die, all the malice he had harbored for me seemed useless.

Surprisingly, Lucifer said that deep inside he was tormented, as nothing righteous pleased him. Believing that everyone disliked him, he became spiteful and could only think of mischief. As Lucifer kept on expressing his feelings, I realized that because of his injury I could not keep on listening to him, as his voice was getting weaker. At this point I felt that saving his life was more important than listening to his apologies. Looking out of the bus shed, I was fortunate to see a police car coming in our direction. Immediately, I rushed out of the shed to signal the policeman in the vehicle to stop. To avoid too much questioning, I was quick to point out that a homeless man was stabbed by someone and needed emergency help. The policeman, seeing his injury, quickly lifted him into the car and sped away to a hospital. Then I was drawn to think of one thing at the time, that Lucifer finally came to realize that hatred was his downfall, and above all I wasn't the enemy, as he had perceived me to be.

*   *   *   *   *

Looking back at some of the memorable moments that I had spent with my homeless friends, I must say that I had learned a great deal from their mistakes which seemed to play a part in their destiny. From Lucifer's steady wrongdoings, the end result seemed predictable for he was put behind bars, and years after this, he was pierced with a knife in an attempted robbery. In spite of all the wrong Lucifer had done to me, it was not within me to keep on harboring hatred for him. However, I felt I had an obligation to ensure that what he had done to me must not be done to any other human being, regardless of their race or religious beliefs. Having an educated friend like Sebastian, I was able to witness how someone with understanding behaves when compared to another who is arrogant or full of hatred.

In retrospect of what had happened to Sarah and Amelda when they became friends with Lucifer, I was able to witness how their demeanor changed and how complicated their lives became when following a man who was delusive. The end result, after a period of fun and feasting with Lucifer, was that Sarah became pregnant and later died, while Amelda and the infant were taken into police custody. Fortunately, Amelda later became sane and was able to spend the later years of her life feeling loved by her grandson and me.

When thinking about Reuben and the affection he had for Sarah, I got the impression that his feelings for her were mixed. Knowing that he disliked begging or being homeless, I could not say with certainty if he was truly in love with her, or if he was sympathetic when claiming that if he married her someday, she would no longer be homeless. Reflecting on some of the unfortunate things that had happened to Reuben, I must say that in spite of his misfortunes, he had the inner strength to remain tenacious in his objective to become a prosperous farmer.

Assessing Julius, it is sad to say the daily use of alcohol affected him mentally, for he usually became argumentative when drunk. Unfortunately, he was stabbed to death in a heated argument while under the influence of alcohol. All in all, Julius was fairly considerate, for I could not forget that day when he willingly offered me some of his wine at a time when I was in desperate need of food, and how he helped me to reach my home when I was weak. It was only when Lucifer lured him with the money he had stolen that he became unfriendly with Sebastian and me.

Thinking about Sebastian, it is unfortunate that after he had experienced a period of misfortune, he became so addicted to tobacco. As a result, he developed problems with his lungs which eventually led to his demise. Apart from this, I remain grateful to Sebastian, for it was from his insistence and encouraging words to do something productive and not waste my youth that I chose not to remain in destitution forever.

When thinking about Alvis, my views were mixed, as I never got to learn how he became hooked on cocaine, or what he truly harbored in his mind. It seemed that as a lonely little person, he wished for something grand or auspicious to happen to improve his status in life. And it seemed that when the moment came that he won the lottery, he probably realized how easily he could have won friends who might have otherwise shunned him. It seemed that after years of being mistreated, he became selective of his friends. I believe the reason he gave me his fortune was that love and respect meant a great deal more to him than money.

To Mr. Bernstein, I remain thankful for the support he gave me at a time when I desperately needed someone to help me in putting my life back together. His show of compassion and respect meant a great deal to me, for I was made to feel important, thus casting away the emptied feeling that I had.

Finally, reflecting on my own life as a homeless person, I am pleased to say that amid the years of hardships I had faced, I did not envy anyone who was more fortunate than me. Though I was occasionally treated with contempt, I accepted the fact that as a homeless person it was imperative that I cope with rejection, since my livelihood at that time depended on begging. Though I was yelled at and treated with scorn at times, I tried to control my anger and frustration, and not say anything hurtful to people. Believing that no one owed me anything, I saw no reason to hate or steal from people. What pleased me a great deal was the show of compassion from some people who offered me a dollar or two to buy food.

Looking back at the period prior to losing my wife and children in a tragic fire, I was very much attached to them, and was selfish in the sense that I only cared about my family and never thought about others who were less fortunate. Being so attached to my family, I paid little or no attention to all the crime, discrimination and hardships many encounter in the slums of Beaverton. In the end, this made me realize that too much attachment was a form of suffering, for after the death of my wife and children, life appeared meaningless. It was not until I became homeless and began to witness crime, discrimination and poverty that I came to realize that apart from my moral obligation to my loved ones, I also had a duty in life to uphold what is fair and to care about those who were less fortunate.

During my years of hardships in Beaverton, I saw no reason to blame the ruling government for my misfortunes. However, an event I cannot forget is when my friends and I were once forced off the streets because a foreign dignitary was coming to visit the city. This was an insincere act on the part of the government to show that there was little poverty in Beaverton. But it was pleasing in the end that after the dignitary had finally left the country, we were allowed to return to the streets to beg. In spite of this unfairness, none of us protested, since our priority was to get back onto the streets as early as possible and not worry about politics.

Finally, I came to understand that my own problems, associated with depression, poverty, and the feeling of being neglected, made it difficult for me to improve my status in life. Over the years as a homeless person, these sad experiences confused my mind with the false notion that begging was the only thing I could do to survive. Fortunately, in the end, I was able to achieve stability of mind and to extricate myself from poverty with the help of friends who sincerely cared about me.

Printed in the United States
130037LV00001B/2/P

9 780595 532063